THE LAST NIGHT

Also by Daniel Gardina

The Lookout and Other Stories

THE LAST NIGHT

DANIEL GARDINA

KING'S MEN
PRESS

KING'S MEN
P R E S S

Published by King's Men Press, Los Angeles
www.kingsmenpress.com

An excerpt from *The Last Night* appeared in another form as "The Lookout" in *The Lookout and Other Stories*, 2012.

ISBN 978-0-615-72012-8

For Kelly

One short sleep past, we wake eternally...
— John Donne

THE LAST NIGHT

Pine and eucalyptus trees surrounded the Westfield Academy baseball diamond, forging a sort of haven where the only sight was dusk overhead. I felt I was somewhere far away in the mountains, in another world entirely, forgetting that just past the trees and through the winding passageways of Coldwater Canyon lay metropolitan LA.

This was a welcomed escape.

When I stepped onto the field for the first time in almost nine years, with that sharp smell of freshly cut grass still warm from the summer sun, I couldn't help but think of all the nights I'd spent here before I left for college. I felt the familiar grind of infield dirt beneath my shoes. My head hung low to watch my feet balance along the first-base line, to see my toe drag across the chalk as it created a white crescent against the earth. I saw myself back when I used to play, fielding grounders at shortstop and throwing the ball to Alex at first. Those were our simple times.

Some part of me still was that person, but the rest knew I could never be the same again. If only I could reach out and touch my former self. I didn't know what I'd hoped to get back. Maybe I just didn't want to know what I do now.

I thought of all the players who rounded the bases on this very soil fifty years ago; how nothing else could have mattered than the crack of the bat, their teammates' cheers from the dugout, the smell of dirt woven in the seams of leather gloves. I could almost see those ballplayers, feel them, before they faded into the evening light, never to return except in memory.

No one knew I was here, especially not Shannon. What would she care anyway? I could have been driving off the edge of the Santa Monica Mountains and she wouldn't know the difference.

No.

I kicked the dirt at the idea. I kicked it again at the thought of her walking away. I'd taken the long road to return to where I'd begun when it was just me, whoever that was, when no one else told me who I was supposed to become. I'd returned to the place where I'd met her. Where I'd met Alex.

My phone rang. My heart jumped when I hoped it was him, that somehow he knew I was thinking of him just then. It wasn't. Then my chest started to burn. What the hell was I doing here? I'd disappeared when he needed me most. Alex had saved my life, and I might have failed to repay the favor.

ONE WEEK EARLIER

CHAPTER ONE

My black Mustang GT sped through traffic, as fast as one can in rush hour anyway, to arrive at Shannon's first recital since earning her master's degree. I snuck in after the show had begun and found a seat in the back just in time. She took center stage in the Ralph Lauren dress I bought her for our last anniversary. With the audience waiting in anticipation, she flipped her auburn curls over her shoulder, then readied the violin under her chin. Shannon stood perfectly poised, almost statuesque, until the hairs of her bow glided over the instrument's strings and Beethoven's "Violin Romance" radiated over the auditorium.

I couldn't think of how many times I'd heard the composition. During the weeks of honing her performance, I'd turn down the volume of the Dodger game on TV, hold still to quiet the groans of the leather armchair, and watch the home team run the bases to the music seeping through the bedroom door. Now, from the back of the recital hall, I could see the patrons were as enraptured as I had been. I may be biased, but she was the best violinist I'd ever heard. Tonight was the first time I listened to the song with accompaniment. The orchestra made her sound even better.

After the show, I gave her a kiss to congratulate her, but her attention was focused on the surrounding people in suits and black-framed glasses. They must have been important because, each time I tried to snag her attention, she'd wave at me as if to say, *One more minute, Ed.*

One minute turned into thirty, then fifty, and then I lost count. At first glance, my suit was just as nice as these people's. Yet I didn't belong. The other musicians and guests who didn't acknowledge my presence only reinforced that fact. They were right that my musical talent might not have matched theirs, but the unspoken joke was that I knew more about their affairs than they realized or preferred. I just didn't have the patience for the snobbery that often accompanied the music business. Somehow Shannon could tolerate the games, even if she didn't play into them herself.

I signaled toward the door to let her know I'd meet her at home, but I doubt she saw me.

My post-graduate life was spent in a cubicle punching keys as resident code monkey for LA's leading consulting firm. When people asked how I enjoyed my job in IT, I said, "It pays the bills." I'd spent the last year developing a database for a start-up Internet marketplace aimed at shrinking Amazon's piece of the pie. I was convinced the client would later file for bankruptcy when it failed to compete, which would negate all the long nights

I'd sacrificed. I regularly reminded myself that the paycheck afforded my coveted, Westside apartment with the creakiest door in the building.

I tossed my keys on the foyer table and strolled toward the far wall of windows. I surveyed the darkened basin below, where the city lights were laid out like stars under the charcoal haze of a sky. I exhaled, weaving my fingers behind my head, relishing my slice of the twentysomething American Dream.

Shannon returned home near midnight. She walked in sporting jeans and her black blazer, the Ralph Lauren draped over her arm in a garment bag. I played solitaire on the kitchen countertop. She strode past me to lay her dress and violin on the couch as I flipped over three more cards, none of which I needed.

"I really enjoyed that."

She spun around as her hand shot to her chest.

"You scared me," she said. "I thought you'd be asleep."

I uncovered the ace of spades and moved it up top to start a new foundation. She slid into the barstool next to mine.

"I fumbled the bridge a little," she said.

"No, you were perfect."

She tried not to grin, then moved the two of spades onto the ace. I didn't know how she saw that simple move and I missed it. She continued, "Why did you leave so quickly?"

"You were busy talking. I didn't want to interrupt."

"Do you know who those people were?"

I shook my head, keeping my eyes on the cards.

"Friends of my advisor," she said. "One was from the LA Phil, another from Baltimore. The Baltimore woman remembered my audition from last month."

"Why don't you sound excited?"

"Because I'm wondering why you aren't."

I stopped flipping cards and collected them back into the box. "I'm just tired. Too tired to even finish this game. Really, I'm proud of you." I kissed her forehead and returned the deck to the coffee table drawer.

"This could mean big things for us," she said. "Have you thought about my question?"

I studied the city lights through the windows. There were fewer than earlier. I hoped that if I concentrated hard enough they would spell out an answer for me. Aside from a line of blinking red bulbs atop a skyscraper, the rest remained still.

"It's just not part of my plan right now," I said. "I want to be sure I have a good job before I start a family."

"I'm not talking children here." She stood to join me, lacing her fingers between mine. "I'm talking us."

We'd been though this discussion a few times. I didn't hate the topic. I hated the uncertainty of having broken up before and what that meant for the future. For us.

Back in college, the last time we were apart, I'd shown up at one of her recitals, very much like tonight. She exited the performance wearing that same black blazer, again with one hand carrying her violin case while the other held a garment bag. When she saw me, some brand of sad pleasure crossed her face—at least I hoped it was pleasure. She decided to approach anyway. Her auburn curls bounced over her apple cheeks and gently tapped her shoulders. They were the same curls I'd once run my hands through—the way she liked it—before I'd smell my fingertips, allowing traces of her honeysuckle conditioner to wander through my nostrils—the way I liked it. The moment was as intimate as it was foreign because it had been banished to another life.

As we walked to her car she said, "I saw you after the show, you know. Standing in the back."

"I said I would come."

"That was before..."

She stopped herself. Before she could begin again, I jumped right in and said, "I want to give us another shot."

I'd never spoken so plainly before. I liked it. I could see her attempting to sort the unsolicited information, but she didn't smile as I'd hoped.

"Ed. I'm seeing someone."

"That Richie guy?"

She gave me a stern look for being cute with her. "His name's Rich. He's nice."

"He sounds wonderful. Does he love you?"

She tried to balance the dress and violin while fumbling through her purse.

"You want me to hold something?"

"I got it. Besides, it's too soon. We've only been seeing each other for a month."

"Perfect," I said. "Best to let him go before he gets too attached."

"You can't come here and tell me you want to get back together."

"You just left. I don't know what to do with that."

"You're right. It wasn't all your fault."

I slowed to delay reaching her car since each step was another grain down the hourglass. My effort was useless, though. Her Toyota was now two spaces away, and the keys rattled in her hand.

"So let's talk," I said. "If you're hesitating for even a moment, let's figure this out."

Now she huffed and looked away. "I can't do this tonight."

That much was true. The next morning was something different all together. After I flipped on the news and threw a slice of wheat bread in the toaster oven, I heard the front door shake. Someone tried the knob, but finding it locked, they rang the bell. I figured my roommate had forgotten his key again.

When I opened the door, however, Shannon turned to face me. I stopped breathing. She breathed heavily, not daring to blink her hazel eyes. I took half a step toward her. She came the rest of the way and wrapped her arms around my shoulders. After a moment, I pulled her to my chest.

Her hair smelled of honeysuckle.

Back in the kitchen, she sat at the counter while I fried eggs and potatoes. We ate with the TV on mute and with her knee pressed against mine.

That was then. Now in the apartment we shared, she was the one asking me to come back, and I couldn't determine what was keeping me away. Knowing what I'd done to save us before, the role reversal knotted my stomach.

"I don't know what's stopping me," I said, squeezing her fingers in kind. "But it's something. I can't ignore that."

She dropped my hands and strode toward the bedroom. She took off her blazer, stopped, and pointed the jacket at me like a weapon. "You need to get out of your head. You paralyze yourself."

"Are you saying I should ignore reason and just say yes?"

My laptop chimed at the head of the dining table: a new e-mail received. I instinctively moved to read it, reacting to the bell like one of Pavlov's dogs. Shannon's face flushed, so I halted mid-step. We squared off on opposite ends of the wooden slab.

"All I'm saying is that every choice can't perfectly match your list of bullet points. I need to know if you *want* to marry me."

The computer chimed again. I knew she hated that sound after hours.

"I'm not going to beg you, Ed. You either do or you don't. I just don't know how much longer I'm going to wait."

She stormed into the bedroom. I wanted to run after her but had no idea what I would say when I got there. Instead, I resigned to silence the computer. I didn't care who sent the message and closed the program. That's when an unexpected name caught my eye.

I reopened the mailbox. One new message, which simply read:

last weekend of my exhibit. hope you can make it. ashley left.   — alex

Since his wedding three years ago, I hadn't heard much more from Alex Evergreen than the fliers advertising his artwork and a couple Christmas cards. The most recent included a picture of he and Ashley hugging in front of their recently purchased California Craftsman, the words "Seasons Greetings" scripted in red across the upper corner.

I reviewed the last two words to make certain I hadn't misread them. "Ashley left." They were clear; yet they didn't make sense. He had friends to lean on up north. Brian and Meghan were part of his new family now. Still, I would have expected at least a phone call if his marriage was on the verge of collapse.

I dialed him right away. His contact held the first slot in my phone book. I saw it often, but clicking on his name created an unfamiliar aftertaste. I waited through the longest three rings before a quiet "hello" trickled through the line.

"Alex? It's Ed. I just got your e-mail. What happened?"

He sounded like a diseased man trying to choke out his final words. "Can you come?"

I stood up. I'd always been unable to sit still during important conversations, but I fought my usual desire to pace in circles over the carpet.

"Talk to me," I said. "Tell me what's going on."

More rasping breaths.

"Can you come?"

I headed directly to the bedroom closet and plucked shirts from their hangers. Shannon, already dressed in her penguin pajamas, stepped out of the bathroom as I pulled a duffle from under the bed. She tried to say something but couldn't. Then it dawned on me how this looked.

"No," I said, "I'm not leaving you. But I have to fly to Seattle in the morning."

"Can't someone else at the office go?"

"The office isn't sending me."

She couldn't fathom what was going on. I told her about the e-mail and the phone call. Her guard dropped. I watched as her expression battled between frustration with me and concern for Alex's predicament. She stopped to compose herself.

"So you go at the drop of a hat for Alex after… what…a three-year absence, but you won't…"

I was glad she didn't finish her thought.

Before I had a chance to think, I said, "Maybe this time away from each other will be good for us." I immediately regretted it.

A look sparked in her eye. I knew it well. She was about to fire off an ironclad rebuttal I wasn't going to like. Finally, she said: "This isn't a problem for Brian and Meghan."

"Please don't compare us to them." I threw rolled pairs of socks into the duffle. "They're the high school sweethearts everyone fawns over at ten-year reunions."

"And we can't have that?"

I laid the bag on the floor and walked to her, scooping her hands into mine. I couldn't tell whether her eyes screamed that she loved me or wanted to kill me. Probably both.

I said, "Alex and Ashley split up after only three years of marriage. I want to be sure about us."

After enough time passed for those words to sink in, her hands finally touched back.

"You're not seriously going tomorrow, are you?"

"I have to."

I thumbed the tops of her lotioned hands.

"I owe him."

She swallowed her displeasure in the way I'd come

to admire. I never doubted how much she loved me. I just hoped she didn't doubt the same. I pulled a hair stuck to her lips and moved it behind her ear. Her smile was effortless. Comfortable. Home.

Then her slight pleasure hardened.

"You may owe him," she said. "But you're sleeping on the couch tonight."

CHAPTER TWO

Alex and I met in high school when we were sixteen. At the first varsity baseball practice for the Westfield Cardinals, Coach McNabb, who was as round as a beach ball and never seen without sunflower seeds in his mouth, paired off guys for warm-ups. Two by two the team broke from the left-field line until this skinny kid, who teetered from foot to foot with excitement, and me remained.

Coach sauntered up to the two of us and said, "Ed Cohen, Alex Evergreen. You're at short. Alex, take first. You better get along because you're each other's go-to guy on the field." Coach spit sunflower seed shells into the chalked foul line, then wandered across the outfield.

My warm-up partner was a lefty, with dark, closely cropped hair that contrasted his blue eyes. He scooped a ball off the ground with his Rawlings glove, threw it up in the air, and caught it again with a swipe across his face. The faded leather and scratched, red "R" scripted over the thumb revealed the mitt to be a hand-me-down. Whatever shape it had once held was lost long ago. That's when he asked, "Don't you feel like the runt of the litter when you're the last one picked?"

"This would be a first," I said, laughing a bit. I nodded toward his glove. "That thing's a pancake."

Pride washed over his grin. "It used to be my dad's. He said it would bring me luck like it did for him. Here."

He took off his glove, opened the web, and presented it like a gift. I slid my right hand inside the warm leather. The pocket felt smooth and soft like lambskin and had the smell of countless summers' use. To my surprise, the construction remained solid despite the decades of wear on the heel and ties.

"Where'd you get yours?" he asked.

I shrugged, handed his back. "Sport Chalet." I didn't have more of a story to offer.

"It's nice," he said. "It smells like turquoise."

I couldn't understand his last statement. He must have seen the confusion on my face.

"Oh, sorry," he continued. "I have this condition. I can sort of see sounds and smell colors."

"Really?"

"It's called synesthesia."

"Syna-what?"

He repeated himself. "I've had it for as long as I can remember. I was surprised when I found out other people didn't see the same way."

I began wondering what it was like to be him, to see sounds. Before I had a chance to ask about it further, we heard Coach yell, "Let's go, boys. Warm it up."

We threw the ball back and forth as Alex backpedaled to center field. When he'd found solid ground, he fired a bullet straight into my glove, stinging my palm through the leather.

"So it's like that, huh?"

I shot the ball back along the same line. Harder. His glove crossed his chest and a plume of dust exploded from the web. Without pausing he completed his turn, ripped the ball from his glove, and flung it back with a smirk.

Our back-and-forth continued through practices, then games. One-two-three innings became the Alex and Ed show. I'd snag a grounder and throw it to first before the runner was anywhere near the bag. Alex then stuck out his tongue and tossed the ball around the infield in celebration. The crowd in the stands cheered.

A month into the season, he and I were packing up our equipment in the dugout after we'd beaten the Knights 2-1. I looked for my parents in the stands. My dad worked long hours at Capitol Records to resolve the complaints of his newly acquired artists while my mom devoted as much time as possible to her interior design business. His absence wasn't a surprise, but she always tried to attend my games.

"Who you looking for?" Alex asked.

His question caught me off guard. I didn't realize my search was so obvious. "The parental units. I guess they got held up." I shrugged it off. "It's not like this is little league."

"It's still nice if they show."

I could feel his eyes burrowing into the side of my head. I didn't want to look over to know for sure.

"What are you doing Saturday?" he asked.

"Don't know. Why?"

"My dad owns a few racehorses. It's pretty cool. We're going to the track if you want to come."

My dad had promised he would help me this weekend with a song on the guitar. He'll probably cancel again.

Baseball had been the only time Alex and I spent together. We got along all right—unlike a few of the guys who thought him strange when he would jam his finger or get hit by a pitch and an odd smile would creep through the pain. They called it his dark side. I thought he just tried to make the best of the situation.

I could have said no. Sometimes I wonder how different my life would have been if I had.

Mr. Evergreen's most promising horse was set to run at Santa Anita Park, a thirty-minute drive east of Westfield. The energy of the spectators rushing the gates felt palpable. Gamblers in polos or Budweiser shirts crossed in every direction. There were a few women here and there, but not many. Once inside, the sweet air of hot dogs and popcorn collided with the firm smell of dirt. Lines formed at teller windows to the left, and far off a bell ignited a flurry of horses thundering down the track. I lost Alex amid the spectacle.

"Ed," I heard him call from up ahead.

I jogged to catch up. "Where are we going so fast?"

"Dad wants to get to the stables to check on his horse."

"Today's a big day," Mr. Evergreen said.

Going behind the scenes, I felt like the racing elite. Alex already looked like a pro, as though this privileged access was commonplace. Mr. Evergreen had insisted we wear polo shirts with our jeans, while he wore a gray blazer and slacks. His broad shoulders and square jaw made him look even taller than six feet.

"How did you get into horse racing, Mr. Evergreen?"

"Call me Jack. My dad passed it on. He used to say, 'Let's go to the park,' so he'd bring me here."

He slapped the *Daily Racing Form* against his palm, then rubbed Alex's hair. I always hated when people did that to me, but Alex seemed to enjoy it.

The stables smelled of wet hay and manure. We passed a line of wooden barns where Jack waved to people I figured were other owners, most of them acknowledging him with a head nod. Two rows down, a gruff man sporting a Santa Anita hat and a clipboard stopped us when he barked, "Evergreen!"

Jack grit his teeth and turned around.

"Carl, how you doing? Nice looking shirt—"

"Your rent's late again. I can't keep feeding your horses if you don't ante up."

"I know," he said, "but today's a big day. I can square the bill in a few hours. I promise."

"A few hours, huh?"

Jack nodded confidently. "How long do we go back?"

Carl's face relaxed a bit. "I can't cover for you again."

"No need. Our luck's about to change."

Jack continued forward. I looked to Alex, who shrugged and followed his dad.

The mustached trainer stood small next to Jack, his red windbreaker and hat contrasting Mr. Evergreen's pressed coat. They talked shop about morning workouts and new shoes while we checked out the horse. Alex said he was a colt—gray with a white muzzle. My head barely reached his back. He shook his mane and stood with the same quiet power Alex exuded right then. I'd never seen him so serene before.

"What's his name?" I asked.

"Daedalus," Alex said.

"What's that mean?"

"Don't know. He came with it. He's pretty cool, huh?"

"Is he fast?"

"You better believe it," Jack chimed in.

Alex approached the stable door. He reached out, but the colt avoided him. Alex stayed firm, moved in slowly. Eventually, the horse settled down. He leaned into Alex's hand to get his nose stroked.

After a few moments, Alex stepped back to join me. As though anticipating my next question he said, "The horse was jittery. I calmed him down."

"How'd you know he was jittery?"

He regarded the question with somber amusement. "You hang around enough," he said, "you know what they're thinking just by looking at them."

The simplicity of his explanation made me smile.

"Excuse me, boys." The trainer moved us aside to buckle the bridle on Daedalus. The horse's agitation returned, and he shook his head to avoid the straps. He snorted a couple times. His jerks grew frantic. The trainer, determined to prove his authority, pulled the horse's head down. Daedalus neighed and kicked open the stable door. He rose on his hind legs. Dirt flew and someone yelled, "Look out."

Jack yanked us back by our shirt collars as the colt's hooves slammed where we'd stood just a moment before. Two stablemen rushed over to help the trainer place the bit in the horse's mouth.

When we returned to the main concourse, Alex looked as shocked as I felt. The vendors continued selling beer and nachos, and the gamblers continued betting while we went from racing elite to nearly trampled.

"How about we get some food?" Jack said while slapping the racing form against his palm. The incident had shaken him, too. He grabbed the back of Alex's neck with his free hand and directed him toward the concession counter. Alex squirmed, trying to break loose of his father's fingers.

While Jack placed his wagers, including a couple of dollars for Alex and me, we brought our hot dogs and Cokes to the field box. Blue canvas separated each section of chairs. Our seats had a commanding view of the track, the crooked palm trees bordering the grounds, and the San Gabriel Mountains only a few miles away. Just ahead, the horses paraded toward the green and white starting gate. I sank into my seat, appreciating the natural aroma of the soil as well the hum of men laughing nearby.

"Why does your dad like horse racing so much?" I asked.

"He says it's a gentleman's sport. You have to make smart choices, know what you're willing to risk. All part of being a man." Alex swallowed a bite of his hot dog. "My stepmom thinks it's a bad investment, though. His second wife hated it, too."

"Two stepmoms?" I didn't mean to say that out

loud, but now it was too late to retract my outburst. "Sorry. It just came out."

He paused before responding. "It's okay. I don't really know this one. She's only been around six months. My real mom died when I was two. It's pretty much just been me and my dad."

The last few horses stepped into the gate. I nodded that direction. "At least you both like horse racing."

Alex shrugged. "I really only like it because he does."

I understood him—for the first time, I think. My dad and I were that way with the guitar. I'd learned because he wanted to teach me. He used to play in bands when he was younger, and though he was on the business side now, he still gave me pointers. I wasn't a musical prodigy by any means. To be honest, I just enjoyed getting some of his free time.

My face must have formed some expression, thinking of my dad. Alex nodded as if to confirm my thought.

"Look," he said, "they're getting ready to go."

The jockeys tensed their postures. There was a moment of stillness. *Clang!* The bell burst. The horses broke from the starting gate. We watched the herd stampede past our seats. The wide charge was hypnotic as the horses funneled into a slingshot around the first turn. The number three horse took the lead only to lose it a few seconds later to one that swooped along the inside rail. There was no telling who'd win.

As the pack came around the final bend, the spectators exploded with exhilaration. The whole grandstand was on its feet. People shouted, "Go go go," and, "Don't lose it now." Jack returned as the horses pounded across the finish line.

"Dammit," he said. "Number five won."

"Didn't you bet on five?" Alex asked.

"They closed the race before I could." He took the seat behind us. "Would've won a lot of money, too."

When the fourth race arrived, Alex was excited to see his 99-to-1 long shot. A towering line of thoroughbreds strutted down the track before number eleven, Speedradic.

"There's your donkey, son."

Speedradic was so small and skinny you could see his ribs. He lumbered across the dirt to keep up with his opponents. Alex couldn't help but find the humor of his wager, especially when his horse wheezed across the finish line dead last.

"Gotta be careful with those long shots," Jack said.

"It was worth a dollar." Alex's tone sharpened to a point. "You didn't win either."

Jack's joking mood vanished. The air between the two grew heavy. Alex looked my direction as though he wanted me to say something, but I didn't want to be the first one to speak. The silence lasted for two more races until Jack's pick finally won.

"Daedalus is up next," Jack said, relieving me of my duty. "Our luck's already changing."

He stood as the horses entered, rubbing his hands together while Alex stared in the opposite direction. My father and I played this avoidance game sometimes. I knew the rules too well.

"Ready to win a few bucks, Ed?" Jack asked.

I'd bet on Daedalus since I didn't know any other horses. I smiled. Answering verbally might have upset Alex.

The jockey steered the horse toward the gate. Daedalus flipped his head skyward a few times, still disliking the bridle. The muscles in the colt's flank quivered. He sidestepped several paces before continuing forward. I tried to preoccupy myself with the horse's movements, as though nothing was more important. Behind me, Jack whispered encouragements under his breath. He moved from foot to foot until the bell finally rang.

Daedalus took an early lead and held it through the backstretch. I should've been more excited since I stood to win some money. Instead, I was busy sneaking glances at Alex. While Jack told no one in particular to save some for the finish, Alex looked unaffected by the surrounding excitement. He stared straight ahead even after the pack left his line of sight.

I saw a black horse pulling up from the rear. Jack noticed, as well. He fell quiet when it passed two, three, four jockeys near the final turn. He twisted his racing form until the paper creaked and several horses, including the black one, a purple number seven, turned Daedalus into a memory. The crowd roared everywhere except in our field box. As the colts crossed the finish, a smirk drew across Alex's mouth.

He turned to see Jack finishing off his beer. "How much did you bet?" The remaining foam slid into his father's mouth. "How much?"

"Enough," he snapped, tossing the plastic cup aside.

Alex cringed in his seat. I should've left to give them privacy, but I didn't know how to excuse myself. Or where I would go.

Jack appeared to be calculating something in his

head.

"I'm going to collect."

He turned in his winning tickets, and the teller cashed him out for two thousand bucks. "See. It wasn't a total loss." He stuffed the money in an envelope. He moved to place the cash in his inner coat pocket but stopped himself, playing some game of mental tug of war. He looked to Alex, who had already turned on his defenses.

"Here," Jack said. "Why don't you hang onto this?"

"Why?"

"Don't let me bet anymore. Money I owe on the stables." He passed the winnings down to his son. "I'm going to check on Daedalus. Meet me by the exit in fifteen, and we'll go see Carl."

Jack had trouble releasing the money. He watched the envelope until it disappeared into Alex's front pocket. He nodded once more, then trudged toward the stables.

Alex signaled for us to leave with a tilt of his head. I followed him through the crowd as we dodged older men saying, "Didn't I tell you it was his day?" and, "Better luck next time." Some announcement blared over the loudspeaker. The garbled sound intertwined with everything else. Every now and then a voice untangled itself from the mob and congratulated another on trifectas and exactas. I had no idea what the jargon meant, but the remarks must have been worthy of the resulting backslaps.

I tried to pick up more track talk, but a quick "hey" surfaced every few seconds to disrupt my concentration. "Hey," the voice said again. I took three more strides before I realized the word was directed at me. I turned to find someone in his twenties approaching us from behind. He wore a Bulls jersey and baggy jeans and swayed to the right with a limp.

"Hey, buddy." He walked right up to me, shrinking the distance between us. "You got a dollar?"

"A dollar?"

"Yeah, a dollar. I need some money to catch the bus."

The guy stood over me. He had dark circles under his eyes and smelled of smoke.

"I only have enough for my bus fare," I lied. "Bad betting day. Good luck, though."

I pushed Alex into the bathroom.

"What was that about?" he asked.

"I'd rather not find out."

A moment later, I looked in the mirror to find the red jersey entering behind us. The only other person in sight grabbed his beer and headed straight from the urinal to the exit. We were alone.

"What about you?" the guy said to Alex. "You got a dollar?"

I caught wind of Alex's discomfort, but he tried to be nice anyway. "I might," he said.

I stepped on his foot to get his attention. "I thought you only had enough for the bus, too."

He looked up at me, but it was too late. He'd already pulled his wallet. The guy's eyes were locked on it.

"Now that I think of it," I said, "I might have a dollar after all."

His eyes widened. "I thought you didn't have any money."

I found myself out of excuses.

"Look—" the guy leaned closer to Alex— "I saw your daddy give you that envelope."

My brain malfunctioned. It wouldn't restart. Alex froze, too. He'd already replaced his wallet. Mine was halfway out. His face was practically buried in the guy's chest.

Alex turned something over in his head. I hoped he wasn't going to try something. Be a hero. Then again maybe I did.

"What envelope?" he said.

The guy gritted his teeth and grabbed Alex's shirt with both hands. "I ain't playing with you." He threw Alex across the tiles, sending him crashing into a stall door. The guy moved in on him. He reached under his jersey and pulled a silver blade that flashed under the florescent lights. "Now gimme the money."

I took a step forward, and he turned the knife on me.

"What are you gonna do about it?"

We locked eyes. I backpedaled to escape. I tripped over my shoes and landed on my tailbone. My spine convulsed from the pain. I tried to shout for help, but my lungs failed. The guy stood over me, his knife thrusting forward. Game over. I was about to close my eyes when Alex leapt between us.

He curled over in a yelp. Collapsed across my lap.

The knife had planted in his hip, causing a red stain to swell through his jeans.

The guy looked around, somewhat shocked. When he found his bearings again, he drew out the blade. He reached into Alex's pocket, pulled the envelope, and ran from the bathroom.

Alex groaned between quick breaths. I didn't even

want to look at him out of fear or embarrassment or maybe guilt that the steel had been jammed in his side instead of mine. He'd taken a knife for me. He'd reacted when I couldn't. If I saw his face I knew I'd be even more shamed.

I yelled to the crowd outside. After no response, I reached for my cell phone. That's when I accidentally caught his eye.

I didn't feel worse. In fact, I could've sworn he was trying to smile.

CHAPTER THREE

Mr. Evergreen spent the next couple months trying to win back the stolen money. He eventually had to sell Daedalus. By the time the wound on Alex's hip had healed into a pink scar shaped like an apple slice, his father went into his room and shut the door. Alex stopped folding laundry to focus on what would be the first time Jack had wanted to talk since the incident.

"Alex," he said. "There is nothing more important in life than finding the right woman to love you." He wrapped his fingers over his son's shoulder. "And when you find her, never let her go."

When Alex saw the luggage by the front door, he realized his father wasn't referring to his stepmom.

To my surprise, Alex's reaction was minimal. Stoic, even. He wasn't one to ask for pity. I tried prodding to see if he was okay, but he shot down each of my attempts, claiming he was fine. He was stubborn that way, or maybe he had hidden reserves of strength I didn't know about. I just knew that once he set his mind on something he followed through.

Yet his new living situation quickly wore on him. His stepmom began going on dates and would either disappear for days at a time or bring strange men home. Soon, Alex wouldn't show to baseball practice and a week could pass without us seeing each other. I needed to show him a good time.

Summer arrived, and on his birthday, I planned to pick him up and do just that.

When I rounded the corner onto his street, flashing red lights lit my path through a cold, June morning. I slowed to avoid the gathering curiosity seekers. I parked a few houses down and walked the rest of the way. As the crowd began to part, I saw paramedics loading Alex, stretcher-bound, inside an ambulance.

I never imagined he'd be the sort to try and kill himself. Alex had filled the bathtub with warm water, lain down, and drawn a utility razor up his wrist three times. The third cut was the deepest. A bolt of pain shot through his body, causing him to drop the blade and kick open the drain. The escaping water pulled the steel down before he could carve up the other wrist. Luckily, the wounds hadn't bled enough before his stepmom broke through the door.

I should have seen this coming. I owed him after what he had done for me, and I fell asleep on the job. Some friend.

Doctors performed a three-day suicide watch before they released him with the mandate that he seek counseling. If his stepmom had seen her ex-husband's kid as a burden before, she was certainly done with him now. He moved into my parents' house for the rest of the summer, and as a therapy graduation gift, I bought him a brown leather wristband that fastened with a wide, brass buckle. The strap covered the forming scars. I rarely saw him without it, and he always wore it in public.

Alex was frustrated with himself more than anything, that he'd allowed his emotions to get the better of him. About a month later, he finally told me what had sent him over the edge. We'd just finished lunch in his room when he said the last thing I'd expected: "I'm adopted."

We both stopped breathing. When I was able to feel oxygen fill my lungs again, I didn't know what words to exhale. He'd found out right after his dad split—well, not really his dad as it turned out. His stepmom didn't break the news gently. Supposedly, his mom, the first one, really wanted a kid but couldn't have one of her own. Jack finally gave in. Was even excited for a while. So when she died, Jack decided not to tell Alex.

I felt I was learning about my best friend for the first time, about a whole new layer even he hadn't known.

"Do you know who your real parents are?"

"At first I thought she made it up. But my dad left a bunch of files behind." He reached in his bag and handed me a packet of papers, the corners faded a light brown. "I found this in one of his boxes."

I read the name on the adoption documents: "Annie Morgan."

"Don't know about my dad. Last known address is outdated."

He leaned his head against the wall and rubbed his temples. His fingers left circular ash marks on either side of his face, so I pointed them out to him. He tried to wipe it off, but the stuff was all over his hands.

"Yeah, it does that," he said.

"What does?"

He stood and crossed to the desk, where he flicked aside a couple charcoal pencils before handing me a spiral-bound sketchbook. I flipped through the pages filled with drawings of leaves, spoons, grapes, trees, landscapes, and even some hands. For someone who wanted to check out permanently, Alex certainly was attuned to the beauty of life's fine details.

"These are amazing," I said. "How long have you been doing this?" I turned the page to see his old house, shaded to an almost photographic precision.

"The psychiatrist I went to was this big art fanatic. Suggested I do art as therapy."

"You're a natural."

"I'm thinking of taking some classes. It's fun."

Fun. That was a word he hadn't used for a long time.

Slowly, the Alex I knew returned. I remembered when I heard him laugh again at the movie theatre. I don't recall the specific film or the joke. His reaction was the important part.

He devoted his free time to drawing, which quickly led to painting, until art became his passion. More than that, creativity afforded him an escape. His use of synesthetic imagery gave his work a unique perspective with explosions of color and texture. Still, as much as I encouraged his talent and tried to be there for him, sometimes he would wander off to be alone, or head to the beach to watch the sunset, not returning until well past dark. I guess, no matter what I did, I couldn't change the fact that he no longer had a family.

That all changed in college.

First, he met Brian in a freshman philosophy course at USC, and they became best friends practically overnight. My first impression of the guy was a mountain of confidence. He was tall, about six feet, with perfectly gelled black hair and the smile of a politician. He complemented his grin with a firm handshake. Even in the first instant of meeting him, Brian had this charming effect that could disarm even the bitterest rivals. Within a couple weeks, Brian knew as much about my roommate as I had learned over the past three years.

There was no confusion as to how likeable this guy was. He seemed genuine—almost perfect. Of course, it was only befitting that the perfect guy was dating the perfect girl. His future marriage to Meghan had never been a question of "if," but "when."

One day before class, Alex and I perused photos taped to the side of Brian's desk hutch. The snapshots formed a collage of family gatherings, music shows, and fishing trips from his hometown of Seattle.

"Which one's Meghan?" Alex asked.

Brian pointed without looking up from the essay he hurried to finish, as if he'd memorized her placement in the patchwork. Alex followed his finger to a girl with green eyes and long, blond curls. She wore a white jacket to shield herself from the winter afternoon, her mouth open in the shape of an "O" as though she were singing, which further accentuated her high cheekbones.

"She's beautiful," he said.

When Meghan returned to campus that weekend, we learned she was an Italian girl with brown eyes and dark hair. She was attractive, yes, but not the girl from the picture.

"Wait a minute," Alex said. He pointed to the singing girl in the white jacket. "You said this was Meghan."

Brian examined the photo. "No, I didn't."

He smiled. "Then who is *that*?"

As if on cue, from around the corner entered a mass of blond curls and a humored smirk that said, "Avoid the pyromaniac down the hall. He's roasting a Styrofoam cup at his desk."

She stopped when she saw Alex.

"That would be our neighbor," I said. Neither she nor my awestruck roommate acknowledged my comment.

"Alex," Brian began, "this is Ashley."

She stepped forward and shook his hand. "Good luck. I hope he doesn't burn down your wall."

As they continued shaking, Brian and Meghan looked on with expectant grins.

They started dating immediately. I told Alex not to get carried away too quickly. He agreed, but Ashley's childlike enjoyment of life energized him like never before.

Over the summers, he'd spend most of his time up north. He said Seattle was a vacation of the best sort: a new and exciting city, with new friends and a new girl. He'd never been part of such a tightly knit group before. I was happy for him. Truly. But I felt as though I'd taken a backseat on this ride.

Before they'd been together for even a year, Ashley

took off her ring and handed it to him. It was her grandmother's class ring, Ashley's good luck charm, which she always wore since she and her grandmother were close while she was still alive. The ring was this antique gold band with rays of sunlight erupting behind the Virgin Mary.

"I want to see what it'll be like," she said, handing him the keepsake.

She held out her left hand, palm down, ring finger slightly separated from the others. A squeak of excitement escaped her mouth, so she bit her lip to avoid any more rebellious sounds. He took a deep breath, looked down at her small fingers, and slowly slid on the ring. She grabbed his face with both hands and kissed him as if he'd returned from a tour of duty overseas.

"When the time comes," she said, "before we graduate, I want you to do it just like that." She gave him another welcome-home kiss. "Will you do it, just like that?"

He nodded.

"Say it."

"Just like that."

He later caught her wearing the band on her ring finger a few times, especially after Brian and Meghan became engaged. For some reason, I worried their relationship would burn out, that maybe they were blazing too hot too fast. Yet Ashley stayed with him over the years, convincing me her interest was more than infatuation. It was only a matter of time before he followed them back to Seattle.

Brian's sales pitch had always been the loudest. "The people are the nicest around, and everything is green. After all, Washington is the Evergreen State. See, you belong there."

In addition to the art studio Alex would open, he could teach drawing and painting at the educational camp run by Brian's family. He and Ashley wanted to raise their own kids in a house with cedar shingle siding and a green backyard, buy a boat to take out on Puget Sound, and he and Brian would play baseball in one of the leagues up there. They were promising him a fresh start.

After college, Alex and Ashley married to the applause of a church-full of friends and family, including me, clapping next to the best man. Alex smiled in my direction to thank me for making the trip to be one of his groomsmen.

That was the last time I'd been to Seattle and the last time I saw him.

CHAPTER FOUR

My plane touched down at Sea-Tac just before noon. Above the luggage carousel, plastic tarps bandaged holes in the ceiling. I remembered the same "under construction" motif from my last visit. The sky outside assumed a similar pattern, with sunlight falling through gaps in the cloud cover.

Green oaks and red maples flanked my drive up the 5 Freeway. On one of our previous trips up the same strip of pavement, Alex had stared out the window and said, "It's really beautiful up here."

"It's a nice place to visit."

"We don't have these kinds of trees in LA."

"Are you kidding? We have those on my street."

"Well... Not as many."

I shook my head. The boy was hooked from day one.

Elliot Bay Gallery sat above the waterfront a block north of bustling Pike Place Market. As I made my way there, roses and raspberries collided with the icy odor of fish. The sun had brought locals and tourists outside to peruse the bazaar for hand-carved jewelry boxes and ingredients for dinner. Their noise quickly muffled once I stepped through the glass doors where yellow posters advertised the artwork of "Seattle's own" Alex Evergreen.

Inside, canvases hung along the exposed brick walls. Chrome picture lamps glowing from above gave a modern touch to the historic building. I felt strangely at home in this new place. The interior's warmth came from the familiar images the dozen or so patrons admired.

To my right, an old lady read from one of the pamphlets. "'His style is greatly influenced by his syn… sny…syna…'"

I smiled. "Synesthesia."

The woman looked up at me, then back at the paper. "Oh. Right. What's that?"

"It's a neurological condition," I said. "When he hears certain sounds, he sees certain colors, sometimes in lines or circles. Or a taste will have a particular shape."

The woman looked as though she'd just been given an unexpected birthday gift. "Wow. I wish I had synath— What he has." She went off to appreciate the art with her newfound knowledge.

I crossed to one painting I immediately recognized. It was my favorite work inspired by Alex's first Fourth of July trip up north. The piece depicted a dark figure looking down a waterline at dusk. Fireworks illuminated people's faces in short bursts of light. Children lit tiny firecrackers with paper wings and watched them zip away like green pixies. Campfires dotted the rocky beach as bottle rockets arched over the water. Purples and greens mixed with red eruptions resembling lattice. This must have been how he saw that night. His work made me feel as if I were that person looking down the shore; as if I were the one who rode that stuffy Greyhound bus 27 hours to see Ashley and be rewarded with fireworks on the beach. Fireworks were outlawed in LA after they caught too many palm trees on fire.

I continued down the wall to find a bronze-colored portrait of Chief Seattle, or Sealth if you cared to be accurate. A totem pole rose behind his headdress and leathery face.

The next painting was one I'd previously seen only half-completed. Its finished form had become Alex and Brian holding the ladders on either side of a fishing boat. They rode the wake, being splashed by salt water, loving every minute of the sunshine. Brian's dad could be seen at the Tollycraft's helm. I wasn't depicted in the painting despite also being in attendance that day. I'd been below deck fighting to keep my lunch down. I remember trying to focus on a stationary object, but the problem was that the clock radio swayed with the rest of the boat.

I turned away from the painting and another caught my eye—one I hadn't seen before but found oddly recognizable. As the brush strokes came into focus, I realized the face on the canvas was mine. A green hue clouded a pensive expression staring at some point beyond the frame. I almost turned to discover what caused such thoughtfulness. I leaned closer to scrutinize my own image.

"You've always looked lost in your head," a voice

said from behind. Alex appraised his art with the pride only hard work could render. "It took me years to capture that scowl just right."

I wasn't sure whether I should shake his hand or hug him. The grateful smile directed at my arrival told me neither was necessary. In that moment, I didn't care why we fell out of touch. People get busy, distracted, whatever. Our three-year hiatus didn't matter because, instantly, we were the old Alex and Ed again. He looked the same, too, save for the tiredness of his eyes. His happiness was also a far cry from the voice I'd heard the night before.

"I sketched this piece while we waited at the airport the first summer you came up."

"You said you were drawing the planes on the tarmac."

He smirked. "Sue me. I just sold it, too."

I noticed the sale tag on the plaque anchored to the wall. The work was simply titled "Ed."

"I'm going to be hanging in someone's living room?"

He nodded. I regarded the concept with honored amusement before the face's dark lines caught my attention again.

"Do I really look like that?"

CHAPTER FIVE

Alex drank his fourth rum and Coke at a darkened Irish pub on Capitol Hill. Patrons bumped our stools as they crossed the narrow floor between the mirrored bar and the neon shamrocks strung across the wall.

"She'd always been so excited to marry me," he said before swallowing a mouthful of rum. "I tried to be everything she wanted, you know? It's my fault she took off."

"This is classic Ashley," I said. "She internalizes everything, nothing gets resolved, until she can't take it anymore and explodes. This isn't the first time."

"No. I really messed up."

"Don't be so hard on yourself."

"You're not listening."

"You want another drink?"

"Ed." His stare grew fierce. "She had a miscarriage."

I stopped mid sip, set down my whiskey.

He continued, "Then she told me she was glad it happened. Glad. And, man, I just blew up at her."

A glass broke behind the bar. The pub quieted for

a moment before resuming its chatter. I didn't know what to say.

"This was our chance to start a family," he said. "To do it right. Now she says she needs time to find herself, that her life didn't turn out the way she thought."

"Where is she now?" I asked.

His shoulders bounced in a shrug. "Canada. China. Around the corner for all I know. She hasn't returned my calls for weeks. I even went to her work, but she's been out 'sick.'"

He flagged the bartender for a refill.

"I think you've had enough, Alex," the barman said, still picking up pieces of the broken tumbler.

"Just the same." Alex slid the ice cubes from the glass into his mouth. "You know, she used to really care. She was even helping me track down my real mom for a while."

This news caught my attention. "Did you find her?"

"We dead-ended around San Francisco. She's gone. Now Ashley is, too." He stared at the alcohol bottles lining the bar. "We're not supposed to be alone, you know? We're social animals. We need people."

"Maybe it's okay to be on your own. What's the point if you can't rely on yourself?"

He glared at me with fire in his eyes. "She's. My. Family."

I regretted saying what he didn't want to hear, then retreated to swirling the liquid around my glass. When I looked up again, French-tipped nails latched onto Alex's shoulder. We turned to see Jacqueline Dane in an elegant, black blouse. She was overtly beautiful. A head-turner. Her chestnut hair complimented her red lips, which subtly angled into her trademark smirk.

"Fancy running into you again," she said. She slid her arm around his neck to hug him from behind. He patted her forearm. "Feeling any better today?"

"I think I'm going to throw up." He stood up from the barstool and disappeared through the bathroom door. Jacqueline took his seat and directed her grin in my direction. "Good to see you, Mr. Cohen."

"How long's it been, Miss Dane? College?"

"That long?" She swallowed the rest of Alex's ice. "You'll save a dance for me at the wedding, won't you, Eddie?"

"Wedding? Who's getting married?"

She looked surprised I didn't know. "Brian and Meghan. Next Sunday. Isn't that why you're up here?"

"Guess they forgot to send me an invitation," I said. "I thought they would have tied the knot years ago."

"About time, right? They decided not to rush until Meg got a handle on law school. Don't worry. I'll get you in."

"That's the last thing on my mind right now."

"Oh? Not a fan of this whole matrimony thing?" She swept her hand across the room in a grand gesture as if the oak-walled pub were a glimmering reception hall. "Spill it. What's eating you?"

"Shannon gave me a deadline."

"To propose?"

"She's done it before. I doubt she's backing down this time."

She scoffed. "Marriage is overrated. Part of me doesn't even want to go next week because my ex will be there. With his new *girlfriend*." She stopped herself. "Forget it. She doesn't even know I know. All that matters is he's going to be there. I know how Alex must feel. He's better off without Ashley."

"Think so?"

"Know so. We second-chancers are survivors. Ashley, on the other hand...she's...well...I shouldn't say anything. We're friendly, but we're not friends."

"I get it."

She delicately reached down her shirt and pulled out a tiny, gold case. She thumbed open the lid and offered me a white pill. "Vicodin?" I declined. She lifted the glass in front of me and washed down the dose with my whiskey. Jacqueline never made quick movements. Each gesture was performed with a controlled grace that made you take notice.

I was glad she showed up. She was one of the few people Alex could relate to on a particular level since they were both adopted—"second-chancers" as she liked to call the pair of them. Her parents died in a car accident when she was one or two. That's how she got the subtle scar at her hairline, as well as her sizable trust fund. She always said it was fine with her. She didn't remember a thing about them or the crash.

A thought occurred to her. "Do you have a pen?"

I pulled a silver ballpoint from my jacket—a gift from Shannon for no special occasion. Jacqueline wrote a number on a cocktail napkin.

"Here's my new cell. I'm heading back to LA next week. It's ridiculous we live in the same city and never see each other."

"You're not staying in Seattle like the rest of them?"

"I hope I never live here again," she said.

"The bride and groom can't seem to get enough of it."

"That's because they like quaintness. I don't do quaint."

I imagined the forthcoming, perfect wedding. I pictured the scenario of Alex seeing his wife for the first time in weeks. Then I pictured the scene it would create.

"Do you know where Ashley's staying?" I asked.

She shrugged. "Sorry."

Alex rejoined us from the bathroom, still shaky.

"You blow?" she asked.

He shook his head. I thought for a moment.

"Where do Brian and Meghan live?"

CHAPTER SIX

T he bride and groom recently closed escrow on a quaint, cookie-cutter townhouse just north of downtown. The two bedrooms edged on the small side, but the crown molding and granite countertops matched the rest of the building's charm. The second-floor living room was ripe with the scent of vanilla candles—their favorite—and a collection of hotel door hangers swayed from the bathroom knob.

Alex perused the books he'd seen countless times. The old picture frames. The familiar snapshots. He lingered on the first image he'd seen of her: Ashley singing in the white jacket. He used to imagine what song she'd chosen. How she sounded. As it turned out, she'd been yawning.

Meghan buzzed around the kitchen preparing three dishes at once. Her red "kiss me, I'm Italian" apron contrasted her dark hair pulled back into a ponytail.

"Look at you being all domestic," I said. "Getting ready for married life?"

She stopped chopping the tomatoes and pointed the knife at me. "Don't give me that Susie Homemaker crap."

I raised my hands in mock surrender. "What's cooking?"

"Chicken Parmesan."

"Smells good," Alex said.

She gave him a sympathetic grin. "Sorry to hear about what happened. It really came as a shock to us."

"Yeah, we just found out," Brian said. "We would have called earlier if we knew."

Alex gave his best attempt at a smile.

"Let us know if there's anything we can do," Brian added. "It's an awkward situation for everyone here, but that doesn't mean we all have to break up."

Like Ashley, there had always been an element of Brian I'd never been able to figure out. Meghan was more straightforward. I respected her for that. When I tried picturing what they would be like apart from each other, I could see Meghan doing just fine on her own. For some reason, I had trouble with Brian, despite his success at anything he attempted. The scenario didn't matter since they loved each other horribly and made their relationship appear effortless. Seeing them relaxing at home tonight, you'd never guess they were the power couple of Mr. Political Consultant and future Ms. Defense Attorney. I could see Shannon and I like them one day, but not yet.

Brian gripped the back of the dining chair. He took a deep breath, puffing out his chest the way a peacock spreads his feathers.

"Hey, I have some good news," he said. "Eric's going to be in town for the wedding."

Alex wasn't pleased. "I thought you two weren't speaking."

"We cleared that up. You know how these things go."

Brian made his reconciliation with Eric sound simple. They'd been best friends in high school, and when Brian left for college, Eric stayed to work odd jobs he didn't keep very long. Brian had never been clear as to why they had a falling out, which was right around the time he and Alex met. Last I heard, Eric was off to Alaska to work in a cruise ship kitchen with no plans of coming home.

Brian looked like he had more to say. Meghan gave him a quick nod before she checked on the pasta.

"I've also asked him to be in the wedding party," he said. "My best man. You're still the best man, too. But Eric and I always promised we'd do this for each other. Now I have two. How about that?"

Alex ran his finger along the edge of the bookshelf. "What does that mean for me?"

"You'll be walking Jacqueline down the aisle," Meghan said. "Instead of Ashley."

I caught her eye for a moment. She went back to stirring.

"You know the history between Eric and Jackie." Brian hit his fists together. "There's still that tension of exes. Besides, we don't want it to be awkward for you either."

Brian conveniently forgot to acknowledge that, in addition to the on-again, off-again relationship with Jacqueline, Eric and Ashley also shared a history. Granted, their arrangement happened before college but not before Jackie, which was why the subject remained taboo. I had a feeling everyone in the room mulled over that fact just then, their panicked eyes hoping that no one would speak the group's dirty little secret. Meghan continued stirring. Brian gripped the back of the dining chair. Alex looked toward the picture frames. Everyone was afraid to say something, so I spoke up.

"What do you think of that, Meghan?"

My question threw her off balance. Nevertheless, in true fashion, she regained her poise. "It's as he said." She stared right into me, hiding any emotion, until I was the one to break eye contact.

That's when Alex turned, instantly calm. "Fine."

"You're not mad?" Brian asked.

"I didn't want to say anything until I knew for sure, but it looks like I'll have a meeting next weekend. With a gallery in New York. I tried to reschedule, but you know how busy they are. I might not even be back in time for the wedding."

Brian looked disappointed before he stifled his expression the way Meghan had done. I wondered who taught whom that technique.

"Good for you," he said, genuinely proud.

"You don't say," I added.

"They're interested in showing some of my pieces."

"Boy, that's great. Isn't that great, Meghan?"

That's when I noted the amount of cheese, the number of lettuce heads, cucumbers, and garlic cloves on the counter.

"That's a lot of chicken Parmesan for two people," I said.

Her chopping slowed.

"We have some family coming over," Brian began. "A little thank you for all their help with the wedding. We'd invite you to stay, but we don't know if there's enough food for everyone."

"Then we should get going," Alex said. He was already halfway to the exit when we heard the front door open and a voice shout on its way up the stairs.

"Meghan? I think I left my purse somewhere around here."

Ashley hit the second-floor landing. She stopped only inches from her husband, her eyes wide in astonishment.

A guy almost as tall as Brian, but leaner, who I'd only seen in pictures, followed closely behind: the new best man. Alex looked to Ashley's waist. She removed Eric's hand and gave Alex an apologetic look of distress.

It must be an odd feeling standing next to your wife's new bed buddy. You sense that you have something uncommonly in common, knowing the rest of the world doesn't share that trait. You want to kick the shit out of the guy, but you can't even move to speak. Only then you understand the structure of a triangle and how much you hate that shape.

Brian and Meghan were equally surprised—not so much at the couple that had walked in, but at the moment they'd shown up. Alex hadn't closed his mouth since her entrance.

I've never been one to control my urges. I found myself giving the girl a two-finger salute.

"Ashley," I said. "In fine form, I see. Sorry we can't stay. We're late for an appointment. Right, Alex?"

He closed his mouth. "Sure."

She focused on the floor as Alex ducked down the stairs. I stared down the new couple until they shifted from awkwardness.

I took a final look around the home. Meghan's knife was at a standstill on the cutting board. Brian might have wanted to act, but decided against it. Maybe he couldn't.

"Enjoy your dinner," I said.

I caught up with Alex between the rows of identical townhouses when I heard pattering on the cobblestones.

"Alex. Wait." Meghan swerved around me and put her hand on his arm. "I'm sorry about everything that's happening. It's complicated."

He nodded, trying to avoid looking at her.

"I don't think she's handling this well," Meghan said. "I haven't had a chance to talk to her much, but— We still want you at the wedding."

He lifted his head. "She wants me to be there?"

Her mouth dropped. No words fell out. "I meant, Brian and me. But I understand if you choose not to come."

I almost told him to walk away, get in the car, and drive.

"I have to get back," she said. "We'll see you soon, okay?"

She sidestepped a few feet before striding back toward her warm kitchen. As she passed, we exchanged neutral expressions like emissaries finished with our negotiations. The driveway was quiet again. I tried to think of how to change the subject. Everything seemed superficial in comparison.

"Why didn't you tell me about the gallery?" I said. "See, you're going places."

The car dinged when the doors opened. He glared at me.

"What gallery?"

CHAPTER SEVEN

T he clouds that threatened rain finally let loose. I flipped on the wipers, and a minute later, Ashley called. Alex picked up long enough for us to hear her cry his name and ask to let her explain, that the situation wasn't how it looked. He never took his eyes off the road. His hand, as if acting independently from the rest of his body, hung up the phone.

The only sound the rest of the drive was the rain pattering on the roof.

In last year's Christmas postcard, Alex's house seemed small. Now, standing before it, I was impressed by the size of the California Craftsman nestled between Washington evergreens. Its stone foundation rose to the cedar shingle siding, and two second-floor windows, boxed with white trim, clung to the sloping roof. This place would be nice to come home to after a long day's work.

"We've been here for almost a year," he said. "Our first place."

Alex's timeline revealed that they'd moved in several months before the Christmas card told me so. Like the wedding next week, I felt the distant sting that I hadn't been notified of yet another major event. These Seattleites lived in their own world that I only tasted in the briefest moments. To be honest, I still enjoyed my involvement, however infrequent. The feeling passed, again becoming petty in comparison to everything else tonight. I almost laughed thinking of all the times their three of a kind beat my two pair.

As we approached, the rain gave a sleek shine to the wooden porch. Alex and Ashley must have been thrilled the day they moved in. I wondered what they did the first night with no power. The image wasn't difficult to hold since, inside, all the lights were off except for the faint glow of daylight draped over a nearby love seat. I always forgot how late the sun set up here during the summer.

Alex flicked the switch to reveal the cozy living room with overstuffed couches and a green-tiled fireplace. Black and white wedding photos lined the wall. The snapshots were artistic close-ups of Ashley's bouquet and the intricate beading of her dress. One showed the couple at the altar. Another caught them in a candid laugh. At the end of the line hung the caricature drawn only a few months after they'd gotten together. Alex's large head and small body ran from Ashley atop a toothy horse.

"Kitchen's over there," he said. "Guest bedroom's up the stairs on the right, bathroom next door. I'll give you a full tour in the morning."

Directly ahead, just around the staircase, I noticed a set of oak pocket doors framed by carved molding, an ornate detail in an otherwise clean-lined house. I closed in to find an ivy pattern etched into the wood.

"What's in here?" I asked.

Alex paused, then slid open the doors to reveal his studio. The walls were blank, but the absence of color wasn't the room's major feature. Everything had been toppled. The desk lay facedown on the floor. Half-painted canvases were strewn about. In the center of the room survived a lone easel with Ashley's portrait in-progress.

He'd captured her nicely: her hair that fell below her shoulders, those penetrating green eyes, her high cheekbones. Yet he hadn't been true to his style. The new portrait was too...ordinary. Good, but ordinary—a likeness you'd expect above the fireplace of nobility. He'd also excluded her uneven smile lines and the gentle scar on her left cheek.

"She cried when she ended it," he said, almost as a whisper. He stared into his wife's painted eyes. "How do you tell me something like that and have the audacity to cry?"

"Come on. We could use some sleep."

He didn't acknowledge my suggestion. Instead, he sat on the edge of a red velvet chaise centered beneath a window. He never interrupted his gaze.

I thought I heard him say, "It's over." I listened to hear if there was more. There wasn't. I stepped forward.

"Alex?"

He yelled. Ripped the painting from its stand and threw it at the toppled desk. The corner punctured Ashley through the forehead. He lost his balance and took the supply cart down with him. Brushes, palettes, and pencils crashed to the floor, and a tube of red paint splattered a line across the portrait.

I wanted to walk closer but wouldn't know what to do when I got there.

Alex breathed deeply to clear his head. After a while, he picked himself up and slowly crossed the studio. His movements were now deliberate, calm, or at least those of someone in shock. He examined the hole punched through the canvas, then gently flattened the tear. He placed the painting back on the easel with its new red streak, nudging it from side to side until it was centered again. I pictured Ashley from earlier this evening, now with the red stain across her face. The paint fit the curve of the scar on her cheek.

I now realized Alex was in shock. In an instant, he stood up straight as if someone had turned a switch in him. All emotion vanished from his face. He strode past me with purpose.

I worked to keep up with him as he stalked around the house. "What are you doing?"

"Nothing."

He continued walking.

"That's not a nothing walk. What are you looking for?"

"Cyanide."

The brevity of that word sent a chill down my spine. He sounded completely unfazed. Rational even.

He headed upstairs to his bedroom. "It's around here somewhere." He rummaged through the nightstand.

"What are you talking about? Where'd you get cyanide?"

"I heard about someone who posed as a jeweler and bought it from a supplier. They use it to clean gold."

He didn't look at me and didn't feel one way or another about what he'd said. Announcing his objective sounded as commonplace as locating his missing checkbook. I sensed my first pinch of fear when I saw that determined look in his eyes.

He snatched a pair of jeans from the floral bedspread, one Ashley must have chosen on a decorating excursion. He emptied the pockets and dropped the pants to the floor. Nothing.

"Fuck it."

He stormed downstairs. He sifted through the coffee table drawers in the living room, among the keys in the hall tree, through the supplies in his art studio. My body was effectively paralyzed, unable to do anything but follow him from room to room. Still unable to find it, he put his hands on his hips as though the poison had gotten the better of him.

Then he slowed a bit, opened the double doors leading to the backyard, and walked into the rain.

I stepped onto the sodden grass. The falling drops were warm, unlike the cold rains of LA. I crossed the stone patio complete with a table and chairs. I caught up with him at the edge of the yard where only a chest-high, wrought iron fence separated us from a two-hundred-foot plunge to the plateau below. Over the trees and past the rooftops, where the clouds ended, we watched the sun sink toward the Olympic Mountains on the most humid evening of the summer—the beginning of what normally would have been a beautiful June night. If I listened closely enough, I could hear the buzzing of electricity.

"You know," he said, "one of the only times everything makes sense is when you finally decide to kill yourself."

My feet wouldn't move. "You serious?"

He licked his lips and nodded.

"What's the point anymore?"

He looked down at his leather wristband that concealed the scar tissue he was once ashamed of but presently considered with amusement. I'd seen his wounds countless times, but now, despite being covered, I wouldn't see those slices more clearly if they were ablaze.

"I thought you weren't going to try that again."

"That didn't turn out so well," he said, releasing a quick laugh. "I never even cut deep enough. Hurt like hell, too. I figured I'd use something quicker this time."

I felt the rain flowing over my head, around my ears, and down my neck like warm gobs of honey. I felt it more distinctly than ever before, which caused a slight twist of guilt in my stomach because I knew my fresh vitality was inspired by my friend's desire to end his.

My heart quickened. My lungs filled with air fresh with pine. The warm breeze carried a certain surrealism I couldn't place my finger on, as if forces greater than my intentions were at work. I felt the universe had aligned to my side.

Alex turned to head back in the house. This time, I didn't think. I just acted.

I tackled him.

The surprise knocked him off his feet. I threw his body to the deck chair and wrapped the garden house around him several times. He fought as best as he could, but his struggle reduced to a squirm as I tied off the end. I stepped back to verify the bind would hold.

The metal chair was too heavy for him to stand.

"Let me go," he said.

I tried to think of what to do now. I'd already completed my entire objective. What happened next was a blank.

He continued rocking side to side. The chair's iron feet thumped against the stone pavers. I dragged the glass table away so he wouldn't break it. Instead, his momentum sent him flying backward, and he landed on the patio with a thud.

"You okay?" I asked.

He stared up at the sky, his face's natural direction. Rain splashed around his eyes. His jaw clenched. "I'm fine."

"You talk about offing yourself like it's nothing."

"Exactly," he said, lifting his neck to look me in the eye.

"Well, I won't make it that easy."

His head dropped back to the ground. After a moment, he accepted he couldn't go anywhere and let out a sigh.

"You finished?" I asked. "Can I lift you up now?"

He didn't respond. I took his silence as consent.

I raised his chair. Sitting upright again, he glared at me.

"It doesn't matter what you do," he said. "I'm not going make it to next week. A wedding with no best man. Former best man, anyway."

My mouth dropped. "What? Is this some sort of revenge? Because Ashley left you? Because Brian and Meghan haven't spoken to you in weeks?"

"You're right. It's not their fault. They have their own problems."

His words lacked judgment. He really didn't care.

"Tell me what you want me to do," I said.

"Forget about it."

I began spitballing, trying to think of anything he'd consider.

"Do you want me to help you get her back?"

"No."

"Do you want to go to LA? Take a vacation?"

"Let it go."

"Quiet. Let me think."

Alex, neither interested nor disinterested, watched me pace as I tried to devise a plan. I didn't know how much good I could do since I wasn't local here.

I couldn't call Ashley—get them to sit down and talk. No, he wouldn't give her the chance. That much was evident when he hung up on her in the car. She claimed the situation with Eric wasn't how it looked, but even if that were true, Alex either wouldn't believe her or take me seriously if I said that was my big idea. I didn't know if *I'd* believe her. Eric's hand on her hip looked awfully intimate.

Brian refused to act. I couldn't call him.

Meghan said all she could outside the townhouse. She was already torn between her friendships with Alex and Ashley. If pressed too hard, she'd be more inclined to side with her best friend since junior high.

Contact with any of them might be too painful for Alex. The inevitable arguments would most likely give Ashley more reason not to come back.

He needed a distraction. A new avenue.

Jacqueline could turn any depression into a party, but whatever festivity she came up with would only be a Band-Aid.

I needed something substantial.

So what do I do for a guy who's lost his only family? What do I do for someone who's lost...

"I got it," I said.

"Come on, Ed."

"Hear me out. Or I'll call the cops right now."

The threat of outside involvement halted his protest. The only thing worse than his first attempt was the three-day hospital watch. The doctors' eyes made him feel as though he were a criminal, and I knew he didn't want to go through that again. I let him settle and prepare for what I was about to say.

"We're going to find your parents."

He rolled his eyes. "I have no desire to see Jack or—"

"No, no, no. Your real parents. Annie."

Alex looked on me with renewed interest—a reflex that betrayed his current objective just before he tried to hide that reaction. For one honest moment, he appeared to be a different person. Invigorated. I'd certainly hit the mark.

"And how do you intend to do that?" he asked. "I've been searching for years."

"I have no idea. Just give me a few days—a week. When's the wedding again?"

"Next Sunday."

My mouth went dry. "Then give me till Saturday to change your mind. If you're so set on doing it, what's a few more days?"

He appeared to genuinely consider my proposal.

"What about your job?" he said.

I was glad he brought that up. I hadn't figured in that part. I blurted out the most viable option: "I'll call in sick. All I need is a week to show you that you have people who care."

He tried to sneak in a rebuttal.

"But if by then," I continued, "you still want to kill yourself..." I let those words hang in the air as I watched his interest thicken. "Go ahead. I won't stop you."

He looked me over to assess my sincerity.

"If I'm not convinced by Saturday," he said, "I can go ahead and do it?"

"I'll even lay your body on the wedding altar if you want." I'd never lied so much in my life. "Just give me a chance."

He pursed his lips as he sorted through his options.

"What if I don't agree?"

My anxiety calmed, and I looked on him with steady purpose. "Don't you want to know where you came from? It's the great, unanswered question."

He glanced back to the horizon, which was now only a sliver of red behind the mountain ridge. Finally, he nodded.

"Say it," I said.

"A week."

"You're sure now?"

He nodded again. "I'm a man of my word."

We shook on it. I loosened the garden hose. He stood up, wiped some mud from his clothes, and went back into the house while I stayed outside to catch my breath.

I'd bargained for more time, but I had no idea how to use the days to my advantage, to fill that hole Ashley had so kindly ripped out. I'd gambled without a safety net. If Alex's thoughts got the best of him for even a moment, I might be helpless to stop him.

No. He gave me his word. But I still couldn't help but fear that all my efforts would only be a countdown to our last night together.

SUNDAY

CHAPTER EIGHT

For hours I tried to shut off my brain. I didn't remember falling asleep or the dream I had. I only recalled standing in a forest at dawn, when the trees blackened in blotches, as if oil had saturated the image from beneath. When I awoke, the sky was still dark and I was parched. I lay open the covers, then crept down the cold, hardwood stairs.

Light spilled across the bottom landing. I followed the source to the end of the hall, where I found Alex sitting at the kitchen table. His fist ground against his forehead. His knuckles were white, his eyes red from restlessness. He twisted off his platinum wedding band as though he hated wearing it. He hated it even more when he *had* to replace the ring to where it belonged.

I retreated upstairs and closed the bathroom door. There wasn't a glass on the sink or in the medicine cabinet. I tried drinking from my cupped hand, but the water dripped between my fingers; so I stuck my mouth under the faucet. The tap tasted cleaner than back home.

In the guest bedroom, I scrolled through my phone

until Shannon's name highlighted. We hadn't spoken at all yesterday. My thumb stroked the call key. I pressed it but immediately hung up. I didn't know what I was thinking. It wasn't even six yet. She was still asleep. I returned the cell to the nightstand.

The same question that had been keeping me awake returned. Alex had already bought the poison. He'd thought about this option for a while. But Ashley only left three weeks ago. I didn't know how long they'd been fighting. Or how long they hadn't talked before that. Or how many times Alex sat at the kitchen table and debated whether to remove his ring for good. Something was still fighting. Something didn't want to give up. I needed to focus on that part of him.

So I concentrated on the task at hand. Somehow I was supposed to find a woman Alex hadn't managed to locate in years of probing. I remembered her last known address from the adoption agency had been outdated. He'd Googled her name countless times. Signed up for people searches and background checks. Cross-referenced leads against pictures he stumbled across, looking for any resemblance to himself. I couldn't spend my time retracing his same steps or hire a private detective. We didn't have the time. I'd bought a week.

I paced the floor. Moving helped me think. There must have been some avenue Alex hadn't tried, some place where Annie Morgan's information existed. Someone must be able to dig it up on short notice. Then it clicked.

I glanced at the clock again. New York was three hours ahead. They were already open for business. I picked up the phone and called a guy I had a couple econ classes with in college, who had since moved to

Manhattan.

"Ed Cohen," I heard through the phone.

"Daizo Saito. I didn't catch you at a bad time, did I?"

"Naw. It's a slow morning. My feet are firmly planted on the desk, and I'm drinking my breakfast. How the heck are ya?"

We exchanged a few pleasantries to catch up before I launched in.

"I need a favor."

Alex finished his orange juice and rinsed the glass in the sink. The first streaks of a hazy blue sunrise glowed through the kitchen window behind him. He found me standing in the doorway and almost dropped the cup.

"I couldn't sleep," he said. "You thirsty?"

I shook my head. "I already had some water."

He tossed me a skeptical glance. I stepped forward, offering a piece of paper torn from a notebook. He looked down to find seven scribbled addresses.

"I called a friend who's a skip tracer," I said. "They track down people for debt collectors, credit card companies, things like that. He basically searches databases of public information. I asked him to look up the residential history for Annie Morgan. Well, Anne Morgan."

Alex's eyes met mine with a renewed gleam.

"He was hesitant at first," I continued, "but I gave him some details on the situation—nothing explicit— and told him how much we'd appreciate the help. It was just a brief search, so he can't guarantee anything. But he found only two names that live in San Francisco.

You said that was where your search took you, right?"

He nodded. "Are these addresses legit?"

"Come on," I said. "I'm a man of my word, too."

For a moment, I wondered whether it was necessary to ask if he wanted to give it a shot. The look in his eyes was all the answer I needed.

CHAPTER NINE

Within hours, Alex and I flew into the City by the Bay on a classically foggy morning. I was a little nervous as we came in for the landing since I knew the SFO runway sat at the water's edge. I hoped the instruments in the cockpit lived up to their design or else we'd be swimming to baggage claim.

Alex was glad I accompanied him. I wondered whether Brian would've taken such a trip. Not this week, at least.

We could hardly smell our rental's cigarette-smoked interior due to the "new car smell" air freshener, which was more reminiscent of burnt plastic than clean upholstery. After a short stint in the glove compartment with no improvement, I threw the scented tree out the window.

The streets were slick from last night's rain. I drove to the first address in the Richmond District thanks to the stack of Google maps Alex printed before we left Seattle. Whichever Annie Morgan had once lived at that location moved on long ago. Scaffolding clung to the sides of the corner building and its half-refurbished loft space. The ground floor housed a dental office. The front window sign, in the shape of a tooth, read, "We're open! Please excuse our dust."

Alex crossed number one off the list. "At least they're not a respiratory clinic."

The landlords of the next four buildings said no Annie Morgan lived there. One elderly woman thought the name sounded familiar, but her memory wasn't the most reliable. The last two addresses brought us to Haight Street. Tourist traps sold San Francisco T-shirts and tiny license plates with names on them. The requisite fashion boutiques, pipe sellers, and other eccentricities were present for such a lively part of town—including a shapely pair of oversized legs, complete with black fishnets and red pumps, kicking through a second-floor window.

A crystal ball with the words "Psychic Readings" hung above our next destination. Alex caught the outer gate as a young couple left, and we climbed the drafty stairs to the third floor. Each attempt hadn't made initiating contact any easier. Our nervous energy remained. With every visit, Alex may or may not meet someone important on the other side of the door. He fought the arresting force on his arm and knocked three times.

We heard someone crossing the hardwood inside. The door opened to reveal a middle-aged woman with matted, red hair and deep wrinkles under her eyes. She wore a colorful, flowing dress with a pattern resembling an optical illusion. Red and blue sheer curtains decorated her apartment, which was hazy with smoke from the cigarette dangling from her fingers. The odor of lavender incense did the task our car's air freshener could not.

Alex took a deep breath.

"Are you Annie Morgan?" he asked.

The woman sucked a long a drag from her cigarette. "The name is Madame Destiny. Or can't you read the sign?" She tapped the plastic crystal ball just left of the door, causing ash to fall from her hand.

"Of course. But were you once known by that name?"

"Who are you? Bill collectors?"

"I'm a friend of the family," Alex said.

She crossed her arms and looked over the two of us, weighing her options.

"I might have been called that."

Alex's mouth hung open. He couldn't force his next question now that he'd found a matching face for the name he'd carried for nine years. He began only to stop himself again.

"Did you have a son named Alex?" I asked.

She scoffed. "You're definitely not bill collectors. And no. Had a daughter who ran off with a tattoo artist from down the street when she was sixteen, thank you very much." She took another puff of her cigarette. "But if you want, for fifty bucks we can consult the ball."

"No, thanks," Alex said.

"Forty five?"

I began down the stairs. "Thank you for your time."

"Forty. I'll even throw in a palm reading."

"Have a nice day," we said.

"Tell your friends."

Back on the bustling sidewalk, Alex looked at the final address—our only "A. Morgan." For all we knew, Alfredo Morgan could answer the next door. Alex shuffled through the pages to find the remaining map.

"It's just a few blocks up," I said.

He forewent the usual exchange, which either meant he'd put on his business face or his nerves were acting up again.

We left the hipsters and walked north. The shops quickly became apartment buildings, which turned into homes all the way to our destination on Levant Street. Alex didn't need to verify which stoop was hers; he knew it at first sight.

The house was a classic, San Francisco Victorian with narrow steps leading to the elevated porch. A rainbow of colors changed at almost every piece of wood—a leftover husk of the '60s Summer of Love amid a street of more prudent sister houses. Alex admired the palette. The painter's feast took his mind off his objective, at least for a moment. He almost smiled.

We ascended the stairs to the red door. His hand lingered over the knocker before he tapped the brass ring three times. The door opened, and on the other side stood an older man with gray hair, a blue sweater, and reading glasses perched on the end of his nose.

"Yes?" he said.

Alex looked at me. I gave him the supportive nod again.

"Does Annie live here?" Alex said.

The old man inhaled, stood upright. "Annie?"

"Annie Morgan."

He looked intently at Alex's face as if the features of this stranger on his porch could reveal his identity. He looked so long I almost waved my hand to break his concentration. Alex stiffened under the scrutiny.

"I'm sorry," he finally said. "She hasn't lived here

for some time."

Alex's built-up anticipation released itself in a sigh.

"But you knew her," he said.

"Yes."

"Do you know where we can find her? Did she leave a forwarding address? Anything would help."

"What do you want with her?"

Alex couldn't convince himself to say it, so I did: "She's his mother."

The man's eyes lit up.

"Alex?"

CHAPTER TEN

His name was John Kemp, a retired botanist, who had lived at the Levant Street house for fifty years. Compared to the colorful facade, the interior was blank. The walls were white, almost gray, the floors a pale oak. Plants offered the only intrigue to the rooms. Potted ferns spread across shadowed corners. White orchids and some neutral-colored flowers I didn't recognize lined the walls along picture rails.

"It's been ten years since she left," he said. He walked his tea to the chair directly across from the sofa where Alex and I sat. A downturned paperback balanced on the armrest. "I nearly sold the place afterward. Somehow, I never could sign the papers."

"Were you two married?" Alex asked.

He nodded. "Eight years. She lived here before that, off and on. We met at a friend's New Year's party. She was a great artist. Painted the front of the house." He glanced around the blank walls. "She even did the inside at one point."

I leaned forward to see if Alex shared my excitement over coming this close. Until now, Annie Morgan had been only a name. A myth. Now we were speaking to someone who actually knew her, even loved her. Alex had perked up when he'd learned his mother was an artist, but the sentiment didn't last. Maybe he focused more on the lack of reward at the end of the tunnel.

"Where is she now?" he asked.

Even after a decade I could see the answer hurt. John said, "She took her own life."

Alex spoke into his chest. "I'm sorry to hear that."

He caught me staring at his leather wristband, and he covered it with his sleeve.

"Why did she do it?" Alex asked.

John sighed. "She was depressed, for sure. Not all the time. But often enough. Part of the reason still eludes me."

"Why's that?" I asked.

"I wondered if I could have done more. She was an amazing woman. Her work always fascinated me. She could see the most amazing colors."

"Was she synesthetic?" Alex asked.

"Yes." A spark flickered in his eyes and spread to his mouth. He looked back and forth between us as if delaying his next question pleasantly tickled. "Are you?"

Alex nodded.

"Amazing. Truly amazing. Do you enjoy it?"

"Sometimes." Then Alex admitted, "But it's not always fun."

"Because you don't have control over it," John said, knowingly. "Annie's was like that. Emotions could make it overwhelming."

"Especially pain," Alex added.

John grew concerned. "So how do you deal with

that?"

"I paint."

John nodded in recognition. He must have been mulling over the similarities between mother and son—at least I was, anyway. He sipped his tea, and a thought occurred to him as he swallowed.

"Would you like to see some of her pieces?"

He led us past the stairwell, down a blank hall, and into a back room. Drapes blocked most of the large windows. He flipped on the lights to reveal walls painted with puffs of colors, like clouds dusted with rainbows. A god with a white beard blew swirling wind from his mouth, beginning in the upper corner and traveling to the doorway. Alex didn't see any of that. He focused on the objects protruding several feet from the walls and covered with blankets.

John moved a dusty easel aside and lifted one of the covers. Underneath glowed a San Francisco sunset. Purples danced with greens and reds across the waters of the bay. The girders of the Golden Gate dripped onto the road below. Blue birds streaked across the sky toward the setting sun as if desperately trying to reach it. Alex squatted and, with his fingertips, gently traced the paint lines his mother had created. He appreciated the crisscrossing brushstrokes of the water. The yellow curves of the sun. He admired them not with pride, but with passion.

He pointed to the bottom right corner where two silhouettes sat watching the magic unfold before them.

"Is this you?" he asked.

John smiled.

"We loved to go down to Fort Mason on the water around sunset. Once—" he laughed a bit, the first time since we'd arrived— "Once she and I brought our dinner there and broke off pieces of bread for a couple of seagulls. But two multiplied into four and eight, and before I knew it, she was running down the beach, flailing her arms to frighten them away."

Alex listened intently, still squatting next to the painting.

"That was the night I proposed" John said, "once we got time alone from the birds."

Alex swallowed, gathered his next question. "Does that make you my—"

"No. We never had children."

Alex quietly groaned. He uncovered a few more canvases. He came across one of a woman with murky blue eyes and dark hair casting shadows over her face.

"Is that her?" I asked.

"The only self-portrait she made." John took in the painting he must not have seen in years. "You look like her, you know."

Alex did. Even from a painting I could see a resemblance. I moved to get a closer look over his shoulder. I stared into her eyes. The way those blues were painted with a glassy vibrancy, you felt they were looking right into you, holding you captive.

"Did she say why?" Alex asked.

"Why what?"

"Why she gave me up."

"It had nothing to do with you." John knelt next to Alex, his voice warming with paternal concern. "She wasn't ready to take care of a child. She couldn't even take care of herself. She agonized over the decision for years afterward."

I thought it best not to say anything. Besides, I didn't know what I could have said to help the situation.

"She would have liked to meet you," John said. "That I know."

Alex turned toward the artwork on the wall. He glanced across the stacks of canvases still hidden under blankets, moving his eyes until they reached the dusty, velvet chair alone in the corner.

"I wish I could have done more," John added. "Maybe she'd still be around."

Alex seemed afraid but obligated to ask, "Then who's my father?"

I wasn't sure whether the grimace on John's face stemmed from faded memories or anger.

"I never liked the guy," he said. "Spoken like a true second husband, I know, but he never treated her the way she deserved. He wasn't a drunk and didn't beat her or anything. He just had his own set of problems."

Alex bobbed his head, looking at no distinct point across the room. I figured he ought to have been more upset by what he'd learned. Mistreating the mother he never got a chance to meet. Possibly being a factor as to why he was put up for adoption in the first place. That sounded like something to be angry about.

He wasn't. He was curious.

"What's his name?" he asked.

"David."

He met eyes with John. "Morgan?" John nodded. "Do you know where he is?"

"Last I heard, he moved close to where he grew up. A small town called Lone Pine. It's near Death Valley."

"Sounds charming," I said.

Alex shot me a look to say my interruption wasn't appreciated. I raised my hands in apology.

"There's not much out there," John said. "He bought some land in the mountains. That's even if he still owns it." He looked Alex over. "You thinking of finding him?"

My friend considered his options. He answered honestly, "I don't know."

"Well, if you do," John said, "be careful. I know it took quite a lot for you to come here for someone you never met. But David is a different sort. I don't know how he'd respond to a long-lost son appearing out of the blue."

I followed John's gaze to a painting resting at the end of the room. Still partially covered by a blanket, the work looked unfinished, of a man's face with granite features. His nose and forehead were rough, like the edges of a mountain, and his black eyes lay shadowed under a scowling brow.

It must have been David.

CHAPTER ELEVEN

Alex insisted we show ourselves out. We knew John wanted to spend time alone in the studio after keeping the door closed for I don't know how long. They exchanged contact information on some old Post-its.

"If you need anything," John said, "call any time."

As we left, just before the front door closed, I saw him carry something down the hall. A painting. John rounded the corner into the living room. He cleared away some flowers to hang Annie's San Francisco sunset over the mantel, then stepped back to admire its new placement.

I let the door gently click shut.

Alex and I walked down the hill toward the pungent car on Haight. A few houses down I asked what he was thinking.

"Thanks for that," he said.

"You're welcome."

"Found out my mom killed herself. I guess it's

fitting that I'll end the same way."

My mouth dropped. "You're not her."

"We might as well head to the Golden Gate. I hear that's an ideal spot."

I grabbed his arm and made him face me. I searched his jacket pockets as he asked, "What are you doing?"

"Looking for cyanide."

"You don't think I'm serious? I am."

"Then take this seriously," I said, throwing down my hands. "You gave me a week. If you want this little excursion to continue, I don't want you to act so casual about offing yourself the whole way. If you pretend what we're doing is a waste of time, I can't help you."

He heard me all right. The fire sizzled out of him.

"I'm glad you did it," I said. "Now you know."

He turned to look at the house again. "All that talk about trying to hold onto her. I wonder if he could have done more."

"There's only so much a guy can do."

"Oh, I didn't mean it as criticism. It's just... I could tell he really loved her. I'd hate to be second-guessing myself like that for the rest of my life."

I settled on saying, "I know," thinking even those two words weren't strong enough to convey my understanding. I supposed Alex saw that, but he let it lie.

We walked the remaining blocks to the sound of the wind picking up. I pulled the keys from my pocket when we were in sight of the car.

"Let's get some dinner," I said. "Then we can figure out what to do next."

I carefully opened the door to avoid oncoming

traffic, while Alex just stood outside the passenger window.

"What's the matter?" I asked.

"Nothing."

I waited for him to elaborate. After another car passed he said, "What was the name of the city David lived in?"

I rolled my eyes. "That's assuming he's still there."

"Who else do I have left?"

"Thanks. I appreciate it."

"You know what I mean."

"You have yourself. That counts for something, doesn't it?"

"I need you to come with me," he said. "This was your idea, remember?"

"I'm aware. But you heard what John said. This David guy sounds like a jackass."

I could tell Alex had considered everything I said, my words merely an echo of his thought process. Despite all my reasoning, he must have felt there was something missing from the argument.

"It's not like I want him to make up for lost time," he said. "I don't know if I even want to talk to him. I think I just need to know he exists.

"Maybe— Maybe it could just be a business meeting, you know? Find out if heart disease or cancer runs in the family. I don't know any of that." He grew more serious about convincing me. "I don't entirely know why I look the way I do. Or think like I do. If I saw him, maybe I'd know there's some history to me. That I had some origin instead of this revolving door of people in my life."

My own words used against me, except more

eloquently stated. I wasn't certain, but I believed Alex fingered the scar from the racetrack. Maybe that was all in my head.

He could tell I didn't want to go to Lone Pine. David had been abundantly clear he didn't want Alex in his life. If he turned out to be the prizewinner I expected, I didn't want Alex to get hurt. Or worse. I wasn't certain he could take another blow like that. Still, there was no use arguing. Alex had made up his mind. He was stubborn that way.

"I need you there," he said, "to feel grounded."

I worked up the nerve to announce my decision. I'd hoped to prod Alex in the direction of LA, where I figured I could be most useful. I also couldn't refuse after he'd given me a week. I stopped struggling and leaned against the car.

"Shannon's going to kill me," I said. "Wipe that smile off your face. Let's go. I'm hungry for dim sum."

CHAPTER TWELVE

L one Pine was a good two hundred miles due north of LA, close to the Nevada border. I volunteered to drive us there because I was tired of rental cars and needed to return home anyway. Alex agreed to the terms.

This was the first time he'd been back since his marriage. Seattle was now his home. I wondered whether he had difficulty visiting the city he'd once escaped, whether the strangely familiar streets resembled somewhere he'd only occupied for a time rather than his birthplace. I just hoped he hadn't changed enough so that every sight that originally belonged to him now evoked the Seattleites.

"I used to bring them here," he said, pointing to the red lights of LAX as we drove away. "Whenever they'd fly back home during college."

"You were always there for them," I said, attempting to shrug off the discussion.

"Like a ritual at the end of each semester."

The airport fell out of sight behind a row of office buildings. He rested his head against the window, while his eyes remained where the runways used to stretch.

We arrived at my apartment before midnight. I opened the creaky door and tiptoed across the floorboards. The moon granted the only light, which was more than enough coming through the far wall of windows. Alex admired the stainless steel kitchen and quartz countertops. Everything was top-of-the-line, but after spending time in his comfortable home, mine felt cold.

A light flicked on. I made sure I hadn't knocked the switch by accident. I hadn't. Shannon stood outside the bedroom door in her baby seal pajamas, her arms crossed. I froze. Alex leaned around me to sheepishly smile at her and wave.

"Alex," she said. "What are you doing here? I mean— I'm so sorry to hear about what happened." She walked over and gave him a hug. "It's good to see you."

He welcomed the embrace. "You, too."

"Please. Make yourself at home. I guess you're here for a few days?" She glanced at me for the confirmation I couldn't give, then guided him to the living room anyway. "The couch doesn't pull out or anything, but it's comfortable."

"Thank you," he said. "Don't let me keep you from anything. I won't be in your way."

She played the friendly hostess without blurting out the more pressing issue I hoped she would suppress a little longer. She moved the throw pillows aside to give Alex more room. Then she looked at me and said, "Can I talk to you?" and disappeared into the bedroom.

Alex gave me an appreciative smile.

"Help yourself to any food in the fridge," I said.

"Bathroom's down the hall. Blankets are stashed in the closet."

He took off his shoes as I closed the bedroom door. Shannon stood by the bed with her arms crossed. I only half-registered her arguments for they were the same ones as before: I wasn't making her a priority; I was willing to hop on a plane for a friend I hadn't spoken with in years; she may be leaving LA for an orchestra job and didn't know if I wanted to come with her. The sad part was, everything she said was true. Even worse, as she listed the charges against me, her complaints were all too reminiscent of what Alex told me at the bar, about how quickly he and Ashley breezed through the yelling stage. Looking back on what he later learned to be the end, there was no last-ditch effort. No significant push to fix their relationship. The conversations just stopped. All that was left was the final hug goodbye and her tearful kiss on his neck.

I didn't want that to happen with Shannon. I didn't want her to stop fighting me. As her voice came back into focus, I knew I didn't deserve the second and third chances she continued to grant. I still craved them, though—particularly when I knew her supply would soon run out. I wanted to prove I was worth her time. So when she asked me, "What do you want to do about this?" I could only answer with what needed to be said.

"I have to leave for a few more days."

She was hurt. I hated myself for doing it.

"Why?" she said.

I thought of Alex's confession behind his house, of the rain flowing behind my ears.

"I'm sorry," I said. "It's not for me to say."

She attempted to duck around me, causing her

auburn curls to whip across her face. I stood firm. I wrapped my arms around her and pulled her close. She didn't hug back, but she didn't pull away either. She just breathed against my chest.

"I can't explain now," I said, "but please trust me. I need to take care of Alex right now. I'll come back soon. I promise."

I felt her eyelashes close. After a while, her hands slid around my back.

Thank God she loved me.

MONDAY

CHAPTER THIRTEEN

I n the morning, Alex waited in the red zone outside my Beverly Hills office to prevent the meter maids from towing my car. I'd rehearsed what I was going to say to my boss, that I needed a couple more days to attend to an urgent family matter. "Be vague but grave," Alex had instructed.

I opened the trunk and dropped in a box of files and binders. I circled to the driver's seat and started the engine. "Piece of cake, but I have to keep up with my client from the motel."

The feel of my leather seats was comforting. I knew my car inside and out. I was now in control. No more rentals. I turned my trusty steed down Wilshire as Alex flipped through the radio presets—Power, KUSC, KJazz. He shut off KROQ as soon as he'd switched it on. After a moment, he returned the dial. Through the speakers came the electronic notes of "Such Great Heights" by the Postal Service, a Los Angeles/Seattle duo. Alex was the first to tell me of their arrangement, how the musicians would send their work to each other through the US mail. And the connections between the two cities didn't stop there.

The comedic morning show currently playing the song was named after the two radio personalities Kevin and Bean. Kevin broadcasted from the main studio in LA while Bean performed his portion of the show from Seattle.

Seattle's MLB team hosted an annual Mariners Cup when a select group of Northwest high school players competed against a team from Southern California. A guy from Brian's school made the cut senior year.

In Seattle's historic Pioneer Square, a series of glass blocks, tinted purple with age, have been laid into the sidewalks. They provide light to the level beneath, to the old first-floor storefronts that became basements when the street level was later raised and paved over. Curiosity seekers can now take guided tours of the Seattle Underground. Walking around our college campus, leave it to Alex to find the same skylights behind Bovard Auditorium.

On a more personal note, his boss from the art gallery was another LA-to-Seattle transplant as well as a friend of Brian's family. That's how he got the job in the first place.

As I merged onto the freeway, Alex asked, "Do you remember your first trip to Seattle?" I disliked his nostalgic tone. He coveted the romance of the Rainy City the way others envied the glamour of LA.

"What about it?" I said.

"I was thinking about your first dinner at Brian's."

"And?"

"Things were so simple then," he said with awed confusion. "Do you remember?"

I now remembered how the sun wouldn't set

until ten during the summer. Light streamed through the picture windows of Brian's parents' house, which overlooked Puget Sound. His place was cozier than I'd expected. From his presentable wardrobe and the way he carried himself, I'd first thought he came from money and couldn't believe both of his parents were teachers.

"Vince is sorry he couldn't be here to greet you guys," Brian's mom had said. "He should be back from his field trip tomorrow."

Alex sat up in his chair. "Guess that means I have a big responsibility sitting in his seat." He rolled back his shoulders, puffed out his chest, and began speaking in Vince's deeper voice. "You're slowing down there, Brian. C'mon. Your stomach's not gonna fill itself." He scooped two helpings of linguini onto Brian's plate. "*Mangia, mangia!*"

The table reeled with laughter, including Ashley's giggle laced with a childlike lilt. If even *I* found it endearing, I could only imagine Alex's level of adoration.

"Has she called at all?" I asked him, snapping us back to the voices on the radio and the cold morning light.

"No. But my phone was off yesterday. Even if she did, the number wouldn't be listed."

"No messages?"

He shook his head. "She doesn't leave them. I guess that makes sense, though. I hung up on her last." His posture loosened. "I'm trying not to think about it."

He was relieved to be back on track. On the desert highway to Lone Pine, he took pleasure in the simplicity of dangling his hand out the window and moving it across the speeding air in waves.

Two hundred miles, four hours, and one diner stop away from Alex's former home, US Route 395 became Main Street in the middle of what the federal Census Bureau deemed "frontier territory." The secluded outpost lay in the dusty Owens Valley between the Sierra Nevada and Inyo Mountain Ranges. Timber buildings, weathered by years of wind and rain, resembled general stores and saloons from the Wild West. The Bonanza Family Restaurant embraced the iconography with their decorative wagon wheels. A giant trout advertised sporting goods. One restaurant's sign was a merry-go-round. The town stood as a refuge for mom-and-pop operations. There was no Starbucks.

Alex rolled down the window. He closed his eyes and breathed in the local aroma.

"The air smells crisp," he said, "like dew."

"I just smell dust."

I couldn't ask my skip tracer friend to look up any information on David Morgan. I figured one favor was enough of an imposition. Besides, if David had lived in Lone Pine for a while, someone should know where to find him. Alex just didn't want to draw attention by throwing the name around. He still wasn't sure how or whether he even wanted to talk to the father he'd never met. First, we needed to verify his existence.

After I filled up my car at the gas station, I found Alex behind the small convenience store. He stood at the pay phone next to a rusted freezer with the word "ICE" in scratched, blue letters across the top. He stared at the open phone book.

"Anything?" I asked.

He pointed to the one listing. "Morgan David A." Seeing the name in black and white, the person suddenly became real. We'd found the same information online before we left LA, but "Morgan David A" printed on the sheer paper held more substance than the computer screen. I immediately wanted to know what the "A" meant.

"Same number," Alex said. "Still no address."

He didn't move, and I didn't wait to pick up the pay phone's handset. I checked the speaker for gum.

"I figure," I said, digging into my pocket for elusive quarters, "if he turns out to be a psycho, I don't want him to have my number. Ah, here we go." I dropped the coins in the slot. Alex tilted the book for me to read the digits.

I dialed.

We waited.

"What are you going to tell him?" he asked.

I contorted my face to say I had no idea.

He leaned closer in anticipation through one ring, two rings, until I said, "Sorry, wrong number," and slammed the phone back on the hook.

Alex jolted upright. "What? Did he pick up?"

"It was a business line. Some guy said it was a hardware store." Alex and I squinted in confusion. "Wait a second." I stole the phone book from him and flipped to the Yellow Pages. I smiled, turned the book to show him my discovery.

TOM & DAVID'S HARDWARE
Contracting - Electrical - Plumbing
"Serving Lone Pine for 20 years."

"Phone numbers are the same," Alex said.

"And it's just up the street."

We hopped in the car and cruised the wide avenue until we found the modest storefront. Large windows bookended the red door. The sign above showcased the name in white letters. I asked, "Do you want to relax here while I check it out?"

He was too nervous to sit and wait.

The hollow *clunk* of the cowbell tied to the door announced our entrance. The shop radiated with small-town warmth I'd not seen in Seattle and definitely never in LA. Everything looked handmade, from the used wine barrels stuffed with rakes and shovels, to the handwritten merchandise tags posted up and down the three short aisles. From the shadowed back room—which looked as though it expanded twice as deep as the customer area—sprung a thin man with a graying mustache and wire-rimmed glasses.

"Hi there," he said. "Can I help you guys find something?"

"Are you," I began, "David?"

"Tom," he said, giving us a pair of firm handshakes.

"Well, I had a 50/50 chance."

"That's the easiest way to guess the wrong answer." He laughed as though he wanted Alex and me to join him. "No, David's our contractor, carpenter, and all-around handyman. He should be back anytime now if you need to speak with him."

Alex ducked into the back aisle, pretending he needed gardening gloves or something of the sort. He knew he could leave me to do the talking; it was the Angeleno side of my personality. However much you tried to resist it, a certain degree of the Hollywood schmoozing, kiss kiss, so great to see you, let's do lunch, of course I care pretense seeps into your interactions. Maybe that came from hanging around my dad and the music business all my life.

"Nice place you have here," I said.

"Glad you like it. We keep it simple."

While Tom and I chatted, I watched Alex over Tom's shoulder. He looked around the store until he settled on some photographs behind the register. Most were of proud customers with their home improvement projects: a new driveway, a chicken coop, a shed. I found one of Tom posing with a happy old lady hugging a sack of birdseed. Then there was a picture of Tom and another man standing in front of the shop. Both proudly raised an arm toward the sign above the entrance. I think Alex saw it, too. He tried to peer closer, but his focus, and mine, was derailed by the sound of the back door creaking open.

Alex retreated to the center aisle as a man in a blue work shirt and brown hair walked from the stockroom to the counter. Tom said, "...we carry various odds and ends, as well. And if we don't have what you need, we can get it..."

I couldn't see the man's face. He slid something onto a bottom shelf and exited where he'd entered. Alex surprised himself to find he'd begun to follow. I glared at him to figure out what he was thinking. His realization was punctuated by the back door opening and shutting again.

"So what can I get you?" Tom asked.

"Rope," Alex said, holding up a coil. He walked to the counter and pulled out his wallet.

Tom stepped behind the register. "Anything else?"

Alex shook his head, paid in cash, and left. Tom's "think of us again" collided with the cowbell on the door.

On the way to the car I asked, "Why do we need rope?"

"That was him," Alex said.

"How could you tell?"

"Who else would it be?"

We rounded the corner to find David pulling out of the alley behind the hardware store in a shabby, gray pickup truck. He drove away from the center of town.

We jumped in the car and followed him past the shops and into the nearby mountains. I hoped the sun blinded him enough so he didn't notice he had a tail.

Once the other houses disappeared and our destination became obvious, I parked on the side of the road below a group of trees. Up on the hill, overlooking a tiny Main Street, David pulled up to a solitary building I dubbed "The Frankenstein House." Even from the distance I could see how disjointed it looked. Partial rooms stuck out like blisters. The color changed from white to red to unfinished. I couldn't determine if the place was a work-in-progress or abandoned.

"So what now?" I asked.

Alex kept his eye on the structure. "We wait."

CHAPTER FOURTEEN

T wo hours passed before Alex tapped me in the driver's seat. I woke from my nap to find day had become dusk. David exited the side door of the house wearing a white dress shirt that was by no means fancy. He twirled his key ring once around his finger, then leapt into the pickup. I started the car, and the secret caravan resumed where it had left off.

"What are we doing?" I asked.

"I'm looking for something."

"For what?"

"Stop asking me that." He eased off a bit. "I'll know it when I see it."

We drove back to town under the streetlights that offered only minimal guidance. David parked across from a dive called Frank's Bar. The name was crookedly painted on a handmade, wooden beer mug, from which part of the foam had splintered off. He made his way inside.

We parked around the corner to keep the car out of sight. Walking up the street, we shielded our eyes from oncoming headlights. They sped passed, and we pushed through the door of the smoke-filled tavern. Blue-collar workers, hunched over beer mugs, lined the barstools of their early evening purgatory. The sunburnt and rough-handed men enjoyed their moment of quiet as they stared at the Dodgers/Giants game playing on the corner television set. There was no sign of David.

Alex retreated to a darkened booth just below a Budweiser logo crafted in a red and amber stained glass window. I held up two fingers to the bearded bartender, possibly Frank, who poured a couple of mugs from the tap without taking his eye of the game.

I slid Alex's drink across the table and raised mine in a salute. "To beer and baseball," I said. "As American as apple pie." We both drank to the toast.

David reentered from the swinging restroom door as a gruff man called, "Morgan, get up here." Alex froze. David sat on the barstool next to the man with the flannel shirt. He slapped David's back and slid him a beer.

"Where you been?" the flannel man said. "Working on that house of yours?"

His buddies laughed.

"You ever going to finish that thing?" the bartender asked.

"Just decide *how* to finish it," another man said.

"Or at least put a fence around it," the flannel man added. "A really high one."

More snickering. Yet David appeared unaffected. He sipped his mug as though he were drinking alone.

The night drew on without incident. I'd grown tired and cut myself off an hour ago. Only the serious drinkers remained. David still hadn't presented Alex with inspiration. The Dodgers lost the ball game.

"What are we doing here?" Alex said. "Let's go."

I snapped back from staring into space. "You sure?"

He nodded and left the booth. He took one final look at his father. Then he pushed through the heavy door.

The car slept just out of reach of the yellow street lamp. I flipped my keys from my pocket, clicked the unlock button. The hazard lights flashed when I noticed Alex was no longer beside me. I turned to find him standing on the corner between the bar and the ride home, his head bowed in thought. He glanced back to Frank's.

The half-lit, wooden sign rocked in the breeze. Just when Alex moved to leave, David shuffled out the door. He disappeared from my view, so I joined Alex to watch him stutter-step across the street, lazily searching his pocket. His key flashed under the streetlight as it dropped to the asphalt. He picked it up, then stood straight at attention.

David was looking directly at Alex.

I couldn't make out David's face well in the dark. I could tell he was squinting, though, probably wondering who was staring at him in the middle of the night in Lone Pine (population: 1700 and one stoplight).

David took a step toward us. Alex stepped back into me. He turned around, surprised to find me there. An instant later, we both heard a sound in the darkness.

A low roar. Intensifying.

We looked back to David. From behind sped a

banged-up sedan. Its lights off. Alex ran two steps and yelled, "Watch out," just as the car clipped David's side without stopping.

The drunk driver and passenger barreled off into the night. Two red taillights flashed once before skidding around the corner. Alex flipped open his phone like a reflex.

"911. What's your emergency?"

"We need an ambulance."

TUESDAY

CHAPTER FIFTEEN

The Trails Motel was a single-level, Western-style inn updated for modern comfort—as comfortable as a rented bed can hope for anyway. The sign's arrow of yellow light bulbs pointed us here. We figured, why not?

Binders and papers were scattered around our temporary headquarters with me in the middle. I sat against the headboard and cleaned up some Java code I'd written while Alex paced between the bed and the TV. A rerun of *I Love Lucy* played in the background.

"You need to relax," I said, without looking up from my computer.

"I'm going stir crazy. Where could he be?"

I needed to work. I was tired of repeating myself, so I recounted the facts without emotion: "When the nurse asked who I was, someone in the background said he wasn't in his room and his clothes were gone. They were very surprised by this."

"Let's go wait outside his house."

I slammed my finger on the enter key. "We can't keep snooping around his place. I don't want any questions from the cops about the hit-and-run last night."

"We'll just tell them we called the ambulance."

"We don't know who this guy is. All he has to do is say that we were the ones that hit him. I'd rather not take that chance, thank you." I looked back to my work, trying to take my eye off Alex's marching. "Occupy yourself with something."

"With what?"

"I don't know. Draw."

He mellowed at my suggestion. He pulled a sketchbook and pencil from his bag, then planted himself on the desk chair. He peered around the room to find inspiration. Soon enough, the pencil began scratching the paper.

"You still an IT consultant?" he asked.

"Yeah. I'm creating a knowledge management database to document and track the client's information."

"And that means what in English?"

"That is English. And stop drawing me."

"Come on. This is the first time I've sketched in months."

"That long? What was your last project?"

He paused.

"Ashley's portrait."

"I say get rid of her. You'd be fine on your own."

"She's my wife. I made a commitment."

"One she apparently values." He threw me a stern look. He was about to speak, but my phone interrupted him. I held up a finger as my boss asked me about the file I was working on. "Yeah, I'm just about to send that to you. Call me if you don't have it in fifteen. Mm hm. Thanks.

"Sorry. You were going to say?"

"I've been thinking," Alex began, pausing to formulate his words. "There has to be something else with Ashley that I don't know about. Same with Brian."

My phone rang again. The blue screen read: "Luis Calling."

"Sorry," I said to Alex, "it's my coworker. If I don't pick up he'll keep dialing me." I answered the phone again.

"I'm sick," I said. For most people, this particular lie offered little room for follow-up questions. Not for Luis. "Yes, I'm still working. No, I can't go to a club tonight. That's not my scene anyway. I'll call you when I get better. Okay. Bye."

I turned back to Alex. "The way I see it, they chose to be loyal to her without asking to hear your side."

This hurt him. My curtness with Luis carried over more than I'd intended.

"Family isn't perfect," he said. "Are your parents doing any better?"

I was initially surprised that he knew of the routine at my house, but we'd been around each other long enough to learn such things, even if our friendship's few-year break made me forget.

When my parents were home together, they remained in separate rooms, often watching the same television program on their respective sets. For as much as they bickered, I was surprised they never divorced. Their relationship was odd, though, because if they'd spend too much time apart or Dad would return from a business trip, I'd catch them sneaking a kiss. They didn't say anything afterward. It was just a kiss. Sometimes they'd watch TV or a movie together. Or read in the same room. They'd return to their normal selves by morning, of course. At least the house would be calm for a night.

"They're the same," I told Alex. "Mom's busy. Lots of homes need decorating. Haven't heard from my dad in a while."

"Why not?"

I shrugged. "No need, I guess. When we talk, it's pretty much all business. I call him about stock advice or homeownership stuff. Chitchat has never been our thing."

"Does he still hang up the phone without saying goodbye?"

I laughed at how he remembered that detail.

I doubted I should ask the next question, but I did anyway. "You ever hear anything from Jack? Or your stepmom?"

His pencil strokes ground harder against the paper. "No." He rotated his sketchpad to get a better angle. "What about Shannon? I hope your argument the other night wasn't because of me."

I stopped typing. Alex eyed me over his paper.

"She'll move across the country if she gets this symphony chair she's been fighting for. Plus she wants to get married."

He continued drawing. "And you don't?"

"My job's in LA."

"So?"

"So we've already broken up a couple times. I just want to make sure, you know? Look at you and Ashley."

"Don't use me as an excuse."

"To be honest, this trip is also straining us a bit."

"Then what the hell are you doing here?" he asked.

I looked him straight in the eye. "I didn't mean it like that."

His face registered a mix of pleasure and guilt.

"So what's your plan?" he said. "She gets the job, you let her leave because you don't want to lose her? You lose her anyway."

His words smoothed over me like an ointment. For whatever reason, I'd never thought of my predicament in that light.

"Maybe you should apply that logic to your situation," I said. "And stop drawing me."

"This is a priceless work of art."

"Let me see that."

I knocked over a binder to snatch the book from his grip. He'd created a caricature of me juggling my computer, telephone, Alex, and Shannon. I liked it, despite the parody.

"Very funny," I said.

"Wait, let me sign it." He did, then bestowed his gift. "Be sure to frame that."

The wall above my desk would be the perfect place to hang an Alex Evergreen original. If only he'd be able to see it during visits.

"Why don't you move back to LA?" I said. "It could be like old times."

He flipped his sketchbook closed.

"We need to get out of this room."

Alex asked the motel desk clerk, an old man wearing a red plaid shirt and Coke-bottle glasses, to recommend attractions around Lone Pine, if any existed.

Built into the hillside above dry Owens Lake,

thirty minutes along Highway 136, the ghost town of Cerro Gordo stood in arrested decay. Mexican founder Pablo Flores' silver mining town was the best-preserved specimen of its kind, according to the pamphlets handed to us on arrival. Among the surviving structures were the aluminum-sided general store, the wooden American Hotel with a balcony stretching across the second level, and the hoist house, once used to lower workers into the mines, now resting as a patchwork of metal walls perforated by rockslides tumbling down the mountain pass.

I wondered how this place once looked as a bustling mining town. I thought of the families who'd called Cerro Gordo home and how quickly those lives changed to create this now-deserted monument scattered among rocks and brush. As I looked over the bullet-riddled saloon, my phone rang again. I'd begun to hate its sound and considered severing my leash to the outside world.

"Hi," Shannon said. "You busy?"

Alex sat on a rock sketching the assorted buildings sprouting from the landscape. I walked around the side of the saloon, into the shade where I could still see his back. I updated Shannon on what we'd been doing, that we'd found his dad.

"That's great," she said. "What's he like?"

"When we find out, you'll be the first to know."

"I have some news, too," she said. Launching right in the way she had, I knew her next words bordered on something important. "A chair opened up at Baltimore. It's one of the best orchestras in the country."

My mouth went dry. "So you've said."

"Ed, they want me. Isn't that exciting?"

"That's great. I'm really proud of you." I truly was. I doubt my voice conveyed the same message. "Are you going to take it?"

She stuttered. "How could I pass this up?"

I weighed my familiar options. "When would you leave?"

"End of the week."

Alex continued sketching. I was certain he was unaware I was speaking with Shannon. He was lost in his own world, completely engaged with his work. I pictured Shannon far away from this barren ghost town. I saw her sitting on the edge of our empty bed, her elbows resting on her knees with the phone pressed to her ear, anxiously awaiting my response.

"This is so sudden," I said.

"I know." She considered her words. "I also need to know if you'll come with me."

"I won't be done with Alex by then."

"That's okay. You can meet me out there."

"Shannon, I've never even been to Baltimore. What am I supposed to do about my job?"

"I'm not saying drop everything and move tomorrow. Because I have to go quickly doesn't mean you must. I just don't want you to take a year or something. Besides, it's not like Baltimore doesn't need IT people. And DC's under an hour away."

My face tightened in frustration. She needed a resolution I couldn't give her right now.

"Can we discuss this later?" I said. "We're talking about moving across the country. I need to give this some thought, and I can't do that right now with Alex."

She exhaled loudly.

"I'm tired of this, Ed. Lately you're more committed

to him than us. Why couldn't this field trip of yours happen next week?"

My face clenched again. "I told you. It's not for me to say."

"The secrecy is getting old. You act as if this involves life and death."

Of course this involves life and death, I wanted to yell. But it wasn't my place. If this whole pact blew over like I'd hoped, then no one would have to know what happened here. Alex could tell whomever he wanted or keep the conspiracy between us. This was no one else's business. Not even Shannon's. I had no choice but to bite my tongue.

"We'll talk about this soon. Okay?"

I could only hurt her so many times before she gave up on me. But what else could I do?

"Sometimes I don't know what to do about you," she said. "I have to go."

The line clicked. I searched for some final words I could have said, but found none.

I slid the phone in my pocket and joined Alex. He showed me his drawing of Cerro Gordo. The sun glinted off the metal rooftops and the hills flowed into the dry lakebed in the distance.

"It's great," I said.

"Just a sketch. But I might be able to make something of it." He shut the book and stowed the pencil in its spine. "How's Shannon?"

His sense of observation surprised me. He'd done this too many times to continue catching me off guard.

"She's moving to Baltimore."

"When?"

"End of the week."

He realized the implications of her decision. "We need to head back to LA, don't we?"

I appreciated his generosity. His offer also annoyed me. Packing the car and returning to LA to make amends was the best solution. That's what we should have done. But if I did what I should have, everything Alex and I came out here for would be for nothing.

CHAPTER SIXTEEN

The Frankenstein House appeared larger just before dark. Rafters extending past the eves stabbed shadows across the siding. I drove up the steep driveway, easing on the gas to quiet the gravel crunching beneath my tires. This was the closest we'd been to the house. I stopped a safe distance from David's pickup truck that had finally returned. I eased the shifter into park, killed the engine. An upstairs light as well as the living room's bay window glowed through the curtains.

"What are you going to say?" I asked.

Several moments passed before that I realized that I'd been holding my breath, waiting for Alex to speak.

"I was gonna mostly wing it," he began. "But the few plans I had just took a vacation."

"Don't think about it. Just go."

He nodded, then opened the door.

I followed him to the front entry. As he ascended the porch, I hid under the bay window. One nighttime visitor was enough; David might consider two hostile. After our door-to-door campaign in San Francisco, Alex had grown more comfortable approaching strangers' homes. He knocked three times.

A deep bark echoed from inside. I jumped, but Alex didn't flinch. Although, I doubt he was aware that he kept rocking from foot to foot. The barking ceased as someone quieted the dog. Still no answer. Alex knocked three more times.

The dog barked again, followed by a gruff voice. "Who is it?"

The question shot through Alex's confidence. He stuttered to find his words.

"Are you David Morgan?"

"What do you want?"

"I'd like to speak with you. If you don't mind."

"What for?"

Alex looked at me, then the door.

"I think I'm your son."

The dog moved to the side window to look out between the curtains. A hefty, black Labrador appeared as surprised to see me as I was to see it. I turned back to Alex, who still awaited David's response.

The deadbolt clicked.

The door opened a crack to reveal David's eye. His body braced the rest of the door.

"What's your name?" he asked.

"Alex."

The admission sparked a shallow gleam of surprise. "You called the ambulance. Didn't you?"

Alex nodded.

"What do you want?" David said. "Money or something?"

"No."

"Because I don't have any."

"I just want to talk."

David looked him over again. "You Annie's kid?"

Alex took his time before nodding.

David huffed. He spotted me hanging off to the side of the porch. He peered as if trying to figure out my story. Dissatisfied, he said to Alex, "Come back tomorrow," and closed the door.

"What time?" Alex tried to sneak in.

The voice said from inside, "Ten o'clock."

We returned to the motel to relax before the big day. After some restlessness, Alex finally fell asleep while I played solitaire under the desk lamp.

WEDNESDAY

CHAPTER SEVENTEEN

A lex was dressed and waiting on the edge of the chair when I awoke. I rubbed my eyes. Once they finally focused, I was surprised to find myself in the motel room and not in my own bed. Just to be certain, I glanced to my left to verify Shannon wasn't there.

We ate breakfast at the Totem Café. Alex chewed his scrambled eggs, and I buttered my toast. The scratching of the knife across the wheat reverberated at our corner table. We didn't make eye contact, or look at the house on the hill we knew was visible through the diner window. We continued our independent thoughts as we paid the check, same when the car doors closed. The morning fog had almost burned off for what promised to be another hot day.

The unfinished portions of David's house appeared more garish in the sun. Their angles became sharper; the nails securing the wood, more pronounced. Alex knocked on the door. We received no answer. Not even the dog barked.

David's truck was parked in the usual spot, so Alex knocked again. As we waited, I could've sworn I heard the faint vibrations of a trumpet. Not only that, I knew who owned that particular instrument.

"That's Miles Davis," I said. Alex turned to me in confusion. "I'd know that music anywhere."

"What music?"

I stepped off the porch and the brass trilled louder. I moved around the sidewall and a drum began tapping. A skeletal frame protruded from the back corner of the house, its floor resting at least a yard above the ground. The music came from a CD player resting on the sawdusted workbench, below which the black Lab lay in the sun.

David balanced atop one of the wooden ribs. He fired a nail gun into the frame along to the rhythm of the drums. He looked strong in his work boots, blue jeans, and plain white T-shirt. His silhouette against the sun was the image of the quintessential craftsman.

The dog finally saw us and ran to the edge of the floor. She barked in our faces, and we leapt back to a safe distance.

"Kiana, sit," David yelled. The dog stopped barking, but she continued wagging her tail while attempting to reach us.

"Morning," Alex said.

David stopped nailing. "You're early."

Alex checked the clock on his phone. "Only by ten minutes." His father didn't reply. "What's this room going to be?"

David fired the last nail with vigor. "A sunroom."

He set the gun on top of the nearby ladder and climbed down. His heavy boots echoed across the plywood floor as he crossed to stop the CD player mid-note.

"Nice choice with Miles," I said.

He looked down from his elevated position to see whether I was telling the truth or sucking up.

"Good guess."

"I was raised on him. I'm Ed, by the way."

We shook hands. His grip caked my palm with sawdust.

"Sorry," he said. "It gets everywhere. Come up."

Alex and I lifted ourselves over the foundation and onto the bare floor. Alex let Kiana lick his fingers as David opened a door that was so well built, its only sound was the hush of a vacuum seal. I'd have to ask him later how to fix my apartment's squeaky monstrosity.

He left the door open for us to follow. The first room could be best described as "in transition." The walls were stark white. Tool chests, sawhorses, paint, and unbalanced piles of lumber littered the floor. The finished portion of the house began at the edge of the room, where the foot of a staircase met peg-and-groove hardwoods. The country-style living room lay beyond that, complete with an overstuffed sofa and large flat-screen bolted above the fireplace. Kiana curled up on the couch below the window she'd startled me from the night before. I imagined she and David spent much time in there watching Sunday football.

Just when I expected the cozy design to continue through the home, the den to my left took on a Spanish flair. The adobe fireplace set in a deep corner explained the partial room extending from the outside wall, which seemed attached as an afterthought. That, too, contrasted the modern galley kitchen to my right. I was almost afraid to see what completely different styles the other rooms embodied.

The sweet fragrance of coffee pulled Alex and me toward the kitchen, where we found David again.

"How'd you find me?" he asked, pouring himself coffee from a steel pot.

"We tracked down Annie in San Francisco," Alex said.

He took a sip. "I take it you met John."

"He told us about Lone Pine."

"And here you are."

Alex didn't know how to respond for a while. The three of us stood around the kitchen as equally ready to have a discussion as wrap up the meeting. I leaned against the wall. Alex ran his finger along the edge of the concrete countertop. David stood with his back to the coffee maker.

Alex began, "Did you know that she—"

"I know," he interrupted. He obviously wanted to leave it at that.

He opened a drawer and popped a handful of Tylenol. That's when I first noticed his bandaged elbow. Last night's shirt was draped over the kitchen table behind me—the sleeve spotted with dried blood and gravel.

"We heard you checked yourself out of the hospital," Alex said.

"This is nothing," David replied. "You want discomfort? Try falling through an ice bridge into a freezing river. This time I'm dry. And warm."

I tried to keep the conversation going. "Do you backpack?"

He nodded. "That's how I got Ol' Red." He unclipped a carabiner from his belt and twirled it around his finger. He'd turned the D-shaped ring, originally meant for rock climbing, into his keychain.

"Why do you call it that?" Alex asked.

"Because it's old and it's red."

"So why do you carry it?" I said.

He debated whether to answer. Getting answers from this guy was practically a test of wills.

"It was attached to my pack that time. I fell, and it grabbed hold of a fallen log," he said. "Stopped me from going downstream. Gave me time to climb out."

He tossed Ol' Red on the counter, punctuating the end of that discussion.

We resumed the same standoff around the kitchen. I was relieved when Kiana trotted in for some attention. She rubbed against my legs, and the corner of David's mouth twitched upward as I pet his companion.

"She's a good dog," I said.

No sooner had I finished my sentence, Kiana jumped to lick my face. My shoulder hit the wall behind me, knocking into a picture. The frame struck the floor and broke into pieces.

"I'm so sorry," I said. "I didn't see it there."

David rushed to pick up the splintered wood. "It's okay." I knew it wasn't. The photograph was of he and another guy, each with their arm over the other's shoulder. His concern made me think the picture meant more than an ordinary snapshot.

"Who's that with you?" I asked.

"An old friend."

David threw the glass in the trash. On the countertop, he reassembled the broken frame around the photo, temporarily mending its appearance.

"Are you no longer friends?" Alex said. He, too, had picked up on David's morose tone.

"Not since his plane crashed."

He slid the frame and picture inside the silverware drawer and closed it. He turned back around. His face clearly said that was now the end of that conversation.

Whatever struggle raged inside him played out across his face. He calmed himself after a moment. This time he spoke without being prompted.

"So what do you want to know?" he asked.

Alex had finally been given a chance to talk about why he'd come here. He searched for a good question. There were so many.

"What's my heritage?"

"Your heritage?" David found the question strange, as though of all the things Alex could ask, this was the one mystery he most wanted answered. Still, he thought a moment. "Well, I'm part Irish, part Italian. I think there's some Spanish in there. And Annie was... Polish, German, and Cherokee. So you're a mutt."

"Did you two have any other kids?"

"No." David finished his coffee and placed the mug in the sink. "What about you? Married? Kids?"

I turned to Alex for what I thought would be a sore subject. To my surprise, he was eager to talk about Ashley. He told David he moved with her to Seattle. They bought a house. She helped him find more information on Annie. Without too much detail, he spoke of Ashley leaving and of Brian and Meghan, how their situation was tough being in the middle, not knowing whose side to take, if any.

"You sound pretty loyal to these friends," David

said. "They didn't seem to return the favor." He passed down the parental advice as if he were an old hand at the practice.

"That's what I told him," I said.

Alex faced off with both David and me.

"They were there for me years before," he said.

David accepted the answer with a nod. He opened his mouth to say something else, but Kiana started barking and ran out of the room. The guard dog turned excited as we heard the front door open. Her nails scratched against the foyer tile. A woman's voice said, "Hello, girl, hello there."

David tensed. He shot around the corner.

"Hi. Who's car is out front?" the woman said. He spoke to her in hushed tones. "Why are you talking like that?" she said. He quieted her again. I think I heard him say, "I thought you were coming tomorrow." Obviously not getting the message, the woman continued, "Why? Who's here?"

Against David's efforts, a pair of tiny feet shuffled into the kitchen. Under the archway stood a spirited older woman with gray hair and a young face, her arm threaded through the handles of a reusable grocery bag. My presence surprised her first, but her curious eyes quickly bounced to Alex.

"Oh my God," she said.

David rushed in behind her. "How about I call you after my company leaves? I'm interviewing them to work at the store." He tried to lead her back outside, but she shook her arm free.

"You are not, David Alexander Morgan." She never took her eyes off my old roommate. "He looks just like Annie."

Alex smiled.

The woman glanced at David. "He is, isn't he?"

He begrudgingly nodded.

She placed the grocery bag on the counter as she said, "You don't remember me. You were only a baby last time I saw you. I'm your grandmother, but you can call me Dorothy."

Alex was enthralled by the news. I couldn't help but feel pride for partially arranging this meeting.

She took a tentative step forward. Then she hugged him. Her friendliness caught him off guard. He soon felt comfortable enough to embrace her back.

"I'm sorry," she said, "I'm just a huggy person. David, why didn't you tell me?"

"They just showed up this morning."

Alex directed her attention toward me. "This is my friend Ed."

I extended my hand, but he slapped it away.

"Oh, come now. You get a hug, too." Dorothy delivered as promised with her strong arms. Then she jumped back when some delectable thought occurred to her. "You two have to come over for dinner tonight."

David said, "I think Alex and I need to talk some more before that happens."

"Nonsense. He's here. You can make it tonight, right?"

"Mom," David objected.

"Come on. It'll just be the five of us. Our place isn't far. Stan would want to meet him, too."

"Just us?" David asked.

"I insist." Dorothy smiled. "How does six o'clock sound?"

CHAPTER EIGHTEEN

Dorothy gave us directions to her home in Bishop, an hour's drive north on barren Route 395. She proposed that we ride with David, but he claimed that he had work to finish and would meet us there.

Over a rustic fence, at the top of a circular driveway, the grandparents' ranch house backed into a surround of pine trees. Although dwarfed by the foliage, the home appeared firmly planted and a natural component of the landscape. The yellow porch lights contrasted the dark wood siding while casting a warm glow over the bronze door knocker.

"Come in, come in," Dorothy said. She wore a frilled apron as well as the big smile we saw earlier. "Stan, they're here."

Inside, the house resembled the cabin my family once owned on Big Bear Lake. The spacious great room—comprised of the living area, dining table, and leading into the kitchen—took the shape of a lodge. Timber beams inclined to the ceiling's highest point like a canopy. A giant, rock fireplace anchored the right wall. White Christmas lights draped over the mantel, above which an elk's head wore a glowing Rudolf nose. The red light bulb blinked intermittently.

Dorothy caught us staring at the summertime tribute to the holiday season. "Oh, that," she said. "We forgot to take down the Christmas decorations one year; so we decided to leave them up."

"How long ago was that?" I asked.

"A decade."

The kitchen timer dinged.

"Chicken's done."

She ran off to take care of the bird. I'd already caught a whiff of the juicy main course. Barbecue. She tended the oven straight out of 1965. The massive appliance looked brand new. In fact, the entire house seemed preserved in time. Unlike the disjointed feeling of David's eternal construction zone, this place felt cohesive. I'd only been here a minute, but already I felt at home.

"Cozy place," Alex whispered. He evidently agreed.

David sat at the kitchen counter nursing a beer. A tall, older man standing next to him beamed a grandfatherly smile at our entrance. He walked straight over.

"You must be Stan," Alex said.

"In the flesh."

He greeted us both with a firm handshake. His skin had the texture of paper. "Hey, I like your wristband," he said to Alex. "Very fashionable."

Alex shyly smiled. David set his beer down and joined us.

"Is this the house you grew up in?" I asked.

David nodded. Stan's face lit up.

"Would you guys like a tour?"

With his gusto, how could you refuse?

He walked us behind the Rudolph wall to reveal a double-sided fireplace serving a small den. A long Tiffany lamp cast a green and white light on the pool table below. Stan said the boys loved to unwind in this room after dinner or during football halftime. He and Alex continued down a hallway, but I stayed behind.

A few hundred records lined plywood shelves. The lacquered case looked as worn as some of the cardboard sleeves. I knelt down to peruse the vinyl collection, my finger dragging along the warm spines. Most were jazz recordings. Louis Armstrong, Count Basie, John Coltrane, Tommy Dorsey, Dizzy Gillespie, Johnny Hartman, King Oliver, and Pinetop Perkins were all in attendance alongside dozens of artists I'd never heard of before. Not even my dad's collection rivaled this one.

"Jazz enthusiasts are rare today," David said behind me.

I stood, slightly embarrassed from gawking at the records.

"We're a small but strong group," I said. "These all yours?"

"And my dad's. He got me into it."

"Same here. Jazz clears my head unlike any other music."

David nodded in agreement. Given his tense nature, I was beginning to see him loosen up for the first time.

"Can I ask you something?" he said. "Where are Alex's parents? His adoptive ones."

"His mom died when he was young. It was just him and his dad, with several stepmoms along the way."

"What happened to them?"

"Jack, his dad, gave him some money to protect once. But some guy jumped us, took the cash. Jack blamed Alex for losing it. He took off soon after."

A frown dropped over face. He rubbed his neck.

"We better catch up with the tour."

I followed him down the hallway, past a bedroom decorated with a patchwork quilt, and through an office where a taxidermic eagle perched on the desk. The back door led to an outdoor Jacuzzi, beyond which Stan and Alex walked down a path at the top of the expansive backyard. A rolling lawn with a few scattered trees covered the double-acre lot. In the distance, the grass turned into rough mounds of dirt, and where I expected a rear fence, the yard opened into a desert of rocks and wildflowers running a marathon all the way to the jagged mountains.

Lavender and rosemary lined the concrete path we followed alongside a stone building. "This is the original house on the property," Stan said, running his fingers over the mortar between the rocks. He pointed to the wooden second floor. "They lived up there, and the lower level must have been a barn or workshop. We found some blacksmith tools they left behind. It's our garage now."

Around the backside of the aged structure stood half-opened carriage doors. Alex peered at something in the darkness inside.

"What are those?" he asked.

Stan smiled devilishly.

Within minutes, Alex and I flew out of the garage on a pair of red go-carts. The engines buzzed like over-stimulated lawn mowers as the tires fell from the driveway to the dirt path hugging the perimeter fence. Alex led the way. I saw headlamps attached to the roll cage above me. I flipped the switch to let him know I was close on his tail. His cart shot forward in a burst of speed. I hit the gas in suit.

We left the yard, and Stan's toys sped into the expansive back lot. Alex cut a sharp right. I swung the wheel to avoid the rear of his cart. Dirt flew. I circled around the brush he'd dodged, then headed back toward him.

"Gotta keep up, Cohen!"

We missed each other again. Our carts skidded in a figure eight like a mechanical ballet. He noticed the same movement. We fell in sync and continued the pattern twice more. I heard his laugh. I'd always found that sound contagious.

Stan and David watched from the grass. I pictured them looking over two go-carts screwing around in the early evening light, piloted by two friends acting younger than their age. It didn't matter. We were all allowed an occasional time out.

Alex pulled up next to me and stuck out his tongue. I couldn't believe he just did that. Taking advantage of his distraction, he veered closer to my car. I swerved out of his reach. "Watch it," I said. He tried again. Our tires ground against each other. The friction of rubber on rubber popped us apart. He laughed, giving up the game.

Our carts jumped tiny hills in unison. "Let's see what you got," I said, then slammed on the breaks. He continued forward while I headed for the dirt mounds behind the house. My cart zipped along the desert floor. I checked over my shoulder to see Alex had taken the bait. He switched on his headlamps now that he was on my tail.

Driving closer, the rough hills in the backyard took the shape of an off-road course. The curved retaining wall slingshotted me along my first right. My cart hopped a speed bump and skidded left. I floored the gas to climb the next ramp. It spit me onto a track several feet higher, where I slowed to give Alex a chance to catch up.

His cart flew around the first turn with ease. Same with the bumps. He swerved to climb the ramp. But when he floored the gas, his driver-side tires lost traction. They tightroped the edge. He turned the wheel toward center to compensate, but it was too late. The tires stuck in their groove until the ground gave way. Then his car fell sideways over the bank and out of sight.

CHAPTER NINETEEN

Stan and David ran after him. Stan moved more slowly, but David charged ahead full speed. I stopped my cart and unlatched my seat belt. David reached the overturned car first. He balanced his hands on the red frame to look in on Alex.

I arrived a close second. David's shoulders relaxed when he heard Alex laughing.

He lay on his side, still strapped to the seat after the five-foot drop. "That was awesome." He had a hard time controlling his amusement. "I hit my head." He found that detail even more hilarious.

Stan helped unbuckle his seat belt. Alex crawled out and stood victoriously over the toppled cart.

"Glad you're okay," Stan said.

He and David rolled the car backward, away from the ramp, and turned it back on its tires. We returned our toys to the garage. Stan closed the carriage doors behind us.

We approached the back patio and on came strings of white Christmas lights wrapped around the wooden pergola. Dorothy opened the sliding glass doors and announced, "If you fellas are done monkeying around, dinner's ready. Oh my goodness, Alex, what happened to your forehead?"

She tilted his chin upward to get a better look in the light. A bump had already begun to show from his escapade.

"A minor tumble," Stan said. "Nothing to worry about."

"Are go-carts supposed to tumble?" she asked.

Alex smiled. "Really, it's no big deal."

"At least let me get you an ice pack," she said. "I know I have one around here somewhere. The boys used to get in all sorts of scrapes."

The ice pack lay to the side of Alex's plate of half-eaten barbecue chicken. I noticed that he and David sat the same way—always leaning forward on the edge of their seats. Earlier I even saw them walk in the same rhythm of quick steps. I never realized how many of Alex's mannerisms I'd memorized until I saw another person echo them.

Alex took a bite of corn. He stopped chewing when he saw a painting on the wall. The family continued telling me about my job's importance in today's marketplace, but I was watching Alex. He focused on nothing other than the framed canvas of a mountaineer sitting atop a summit, pack strapped on, surveying the cloud cover below. He rose to examine the art more closely.

"Is this Annie's?" he asked.

"Yes," Dorothy said. "How did you know?"

"I can tell by the style."

"So you have seen her work."

"Only recently."

"That's David in the picture," she said.

David rolled his eyes the way children do when they're sick of their parents boasting about them.

"It's one of my favorites," she continued. "Annie had this fantastic eye. It was something about the way she saw things. I can't remember what it was called."

"Synesthesia," Alex said.

"Yes, that's it."

He smiled to see David and Stan listening from across the table. "I have it, too."

"That's fascinating. When did you realize you had this?"

"Doctors diagnosed me when I was nine, but I've had it for as long as I remember. I was kind of surprised to learn everyone else didn't see the same way."

"What does it feel like?" she asked.

"Oh, come on, Dorothy," Stan said. "This isn't an interrogation."

"I'm sorry." She obviously didn't want to stop. "You must think I'm crazy for asking so many questions."

Alex laughed. "Not at all. Ashley was even more curious when she first found out."

"Ashley?" Stan asked.

The energy Alex had been building instantly deflated as if he only now remembered what that name meant. His shoulders sunk in on themselves, and he forgot how to blink.

"His wife," I said.

"Wife?" Dorothy lit up. "You didn't tell me you were married. Do I have great grandkids I don't know about?"

Alex tossed a glance my way to tell me not to say anything.

"No kids," he said. "I wanted a couple someday."

"Why do you say it like that?" she asked, genuinely concerned. Everything Dorothy said was sincere. I think that was why her presence was so refreshing.

Alex said, "Because we might not get back together."

"Then why are you smiling?" Stan asked.

The question made Alex smile even more. He relished the private thought a moment longer before he shared.

"I was just thinking of something she said one night. We'd been dating for about six months at the time. We were in Seattle, and she drove us back from dinner—it was an Italian restaurant called Machiavelli's—when I told her that I wanted to do something great with my life—I can't believe I'm repeating this—that, I wanted to be a hero of some kind. Without hesitation she said, 'Be a father.'

"I immediately knew how serious she was because hers left when she was eight. Her mom raised her alone." He turned away from David as though uncomfortable with their accidental eye contact. "Even if we never speak again, I'll always admire her for that moment. She made me want to be that father.

"I just wish it were with her."

The Morgans all turned sympathetic eyes on Alex. Even David managed a certain degree of concern.

"Well," Dorothy began, "if you truly care about someone, that's all that matters. You find a way to make it work."

Her hand slid over Stan's fingers. He responded in

kind. Their touch communicated an understanding, perhaps of a past obstacle (or several) overcome through fifty or so years of marriage. That amount of time was humbling. Imagining what those mended wounds could have been was equally calming. An inkling of hope surfaced in me just to know a relationship could survive those trials. As I opened my mouth to ask her to elaborate, my cell phone killed the moment.

"Sorry," I said. "I thought I turned it off." I was about to do just that, but the screen showed a 206 area code. I didn't recognize the Seattle number. Ashley, maybe?

I excused myself and exited through the sliding doors onto the patio. The strings of white lights glimmered overhead. I paid attention to the number of rings so the call didn't go to voicemail. I closed the door behind me.

"Hello?"

"*Bonjour*, Eddie."

My tension sank. "Jacqueline?"

"You sound surprised."

"I just didn't recognize the number."

"I gave you my new cell at the bar."

"Right. I haven't programmed that yet."

"You and Alex want to get together tonight? I figure he's got to be with you after you two just up and vanished. Everybody's been wondering what happened."

She sparked my interest. "Who's been wondering?"

"Meghan, Brian, Ashley, the pope."

"We haven't gotten any calls."

"Alex should check his voicemail," she said. "Anyway, tonight, what do you say?"

"We're not in Seattle."

"I'm not either, silly. I had to get out of there. I'm back in LA for a couple days."

Her parents leaving her that trust fund definitely had its benefits.

"We're not in LA either," I said, breaking her enthusiasm.

"Then where the hell are you?"

"We're in Lone Pine. Well, Bishop right now."

"Bishop? Isn't that in the middle of nowhere?"

"Let me call you later."

"Okay. You coming back for the wedding on Sunday?"

I seriously considered that question.

"Hope so."

As soon as I hung up, I switched my phone to silent. As soon as I did that, the blue screen started flashing again. "Luis Calling." Some coworkers should just stay at work. I sent him to voicemail.

A pair of headlights lit up the old stone garage to my left. The brightened driveway returned to darkness, and I heard a car door close. A tall man with sandy blond hair and a goatee, wearing slacks and a dress shirt, rounded the corner. His stride never broke despite his obvious surprise at finding me there.

"Hi," he said.

"Hey. I'm Ed."

He shook my hand. He opened his mouth to say his name but stopped when he saw the dinner party inside. He forgot about me. The table conversation ceased when he opened the door and stepped inside, with me close behind.

"Matt, honey," Dorothy said, "what a surprise."

She and Stan were pleased to see their visitor. David squirmed in his chair.

"Sorry." David stood up from the table. "I didn't think you'd be here."

"Likewise," Matt said.

Dorothy went into the kitchen to play the gracious hostess. "We have some chicken and beans and corn if you're hungry." She grabbed him a plate.

Matt scanned the room. His eyes landed on Alex. They narrowed as though he recognized him from somewhere.

"Who are our guests?" he asked.

Dorothy and Stan were hesitant to reply. I'd already introduced myself. David reluctantly took on the responsibility.

"This is Alex," he said, "and behind you is Ed. They're visiting from out of town."

A note of suspicious revelation swept over Matt.

David motioned to Alex. "This is Annie's kid."

Matt nodded once. Then he punched David in the face.

CHAPTER TWENTY

David fell backward over his chair, sending he and the furniture crashing onto the rug. I stood frozen. Stan and Dorothy yelled, "Matthew," as he shook the pain from his hand.

I expected David to retaliate. Instead, he accepted his punishment. Blood trickled from his nose.

"Forgive me." The assailant offered his hand to Alex. "I'm Matt." He tilted his head to David. "That's my brother."

Alex's eyes widened with disbelief. I almost laughed.

"Matthew," Dorothy said, "get in the kitchen and do the dishes."

David rose to his feet and gently touched his nose. "I don't think it's broken."

"Let me get another ice pack," she said, appraising the damage.

Neither Matt nor Dorothy looked at each other as they crossed paths on their respective routes. Familial stubbornness or determination, maybe? Now I saw where Alex got it. Stan and Alex helped David into the bathroom around the corner, leaving me as the lone survivor of the dining room brawl. I headed toward the backyard to get some air.

"Wait."

Matt's word stopped me.

"Sorry about that," he said. "I'm—"

"Matt. I heard. Ed."

"Right. Ed. Sorry you had to see that. It goes back a long way between us."

"That's some sibling rivalry."

"Something like that." Matt removed the greasy broiling pan from the counter and slid it in the sink. He turned on the water, rolled up his sleeves. "So how do you know Alex?"

"High school. And college."

I settled onto a barstool at the kitchen counter as Dorothy shuffled around the corner. She crushed an ice pack in her hands and pointed it at Matt. "You should be ashamed of yourself. You two need to get over this thing." She continued into the bathroom without breaking her pace.

"Sorry," he called after her. "It was the way he—"

Matt cut himself short, as though his reason didn't excuse his behavior. He unleashed his frustration through scrubbing. He placed the top half of the pan on the counter, but the soapy film made it slip to the floor with a *clang*. He gritted his teeth and slammed his hands onto his hips.

I slid from the barstool, grabbed a dish towel, and picked up the sheet from the linoleum. "Let me help."

"You don't have to do that," he said.

"I get antsy if I'm not doing anything. Keep washing. It'll help you blow off steam."

"Right."

"Just be more careful with the glass."

Matt let out a chuckle. He cleaned the bottom half of the pan in pensive circles. When he finished, he passed it to me to dry. We were a regular assembly line.

"How was your evening before I got here?" he asked.

"Good. Tried out the go-carts."

He perked up. "Took them for a nice spin, huh?"

"Alex spun more than I did."

Matt, scrubbing the wooden salad tongs, turned his head toward the bathroom. We were unable to see anything from this angle.

"He sure looks like her," he said in amazement. "Annie."

"So we've heard."

"Did he..." Matt trailed off. He focused his attention on rinsing the salad spoon. "Did he ever get to meet her?"

"No." I took the wooden handle from him. "This whole birth family thing is sort of new to us."

Just then, Alex returned from the bathroom.

"David will be fine," he said.

Matt stopped washing to look at Alex. He leaned his back against the sink, palms on the countertop. He regarded my friend with somber pleasure.

"It's nice to finally meet you," he said.

Alex was uncertain as to why he received the extra attention.

"So you're my uncle."

Matt forced a smile. "Guess so."

"You knew my mother?"

"We were good friends."

Alex chewed his words before he asked, "What was she like?"

Matt took a deep breath as he considered his response.

"She was complicated. She suffered from depression, which was ultimately why she—"

"Killed herself," Alex said. "I know."

Matt picked up a towel to dry his hands. "I was going to say put you up for adoption."

Alex accepted the correction. He relaxed again.

"But about certain things," Matt continued, "she was the most confident person I knew. I guess she was sort of a paradox that way."

"What was she confident about?" he asked.

"Her art, mostly. Herself half the time. She had this inner strength she often forgot about." Matt paused to remember the specifics of some distant moment as he fingered the corners of the dish towel. "I don't know if it means anything now, but she tried her best to raise you. She hated giving you up."

Alex swallowed. He looked at the clock on the ancient stove. "We should get going."

I finished drying the salad tongs. Matt tossed the towel on the counter and walked us to the front door. He gave us a big smile and shook our hands.

"If you need anything while you're here, just let us know."

On the ride home, my earlier conversation with Jacqueline nagged at me. I asked Alex if his wife had called at all. He said she hadn't. The delay before his answer wasn't convincing.

THURSDAY

CHAPTER TWENTY-ONE

The morning began cooler than usual. Light cloud cover offered a welcomed reprieve from the sun's line of fire. On our way to breakfast at the Totem Café, we spotted David's truck outside the hardware store. Alex suggested we stop by to check on him.

The cowbell hanging from the front door clunked as we stepped inside. Behind the cash register, Tom read the newspaper over his wire-rimmed glasses. "Gentlemen," he said, swinging his legs off the counter. "Nice to see you again. Figure out what else you need?" He set down the paper to give us his full attention.

"Actually, we hoped to speak with David," Alex said.

"Fair enough. David," he called to the back room, "you have customers."

David appeared from the stockroom wearing cargo pants and a lightweight fleece. He asked Tom if they had any laces left in stock, but he stopped when he saw us.

"Morning," Alex said.

Tom looked back and forth between David and

Alex. He lifted a package of bootlaces from a spinning display next to the register and slid them over.

Alex continued, "We just wanted to check in to see how you were after last night."

"Fine. I'm just on my way out."

He tossed the laces on top of something sitting on the floor behind the counter. A couple of nylon straps dangled into the aisle.

"What's the backpack for?" I asked.

He looked at the bag as if to say, *What? This backpack?*

"Thought I'd get some time in on the hill," he said.

"That big one over there?" Alex said.

"If you mean Mount Whitney, then no. It's too late in the day to start up that. Plus I think I'll take it easy this climb. I'm still a little sore from the other night with the whole car running me over thing."

"*That's* what happened?" Tom said.

Alex didn't hesitate to ask, "Can we come?"

Pressured answers definitely weren't David's specialty. Tom noticed his business partner's discomfort. He looked in his coffee mug, pursed his lips and graying mustache, and said, "Would you look at that? I need me some more joe." He excused himself to the rear of the store.

David now stood alone. He looked over his newfound son. "You ever climbed before?"

"I live in Seattle. We're outside as long as possible the moment the rain lets up."

I shot Alex a puzzled expression. I knew he'd been hiking at least once when I went with he, Ashley, and crew several years ago—the entirety of my backwoods experience—but as far as I knew, he wasn't a Mount

Rainier enthusiast.

"I'm no expert," he continued, "but I can hold my own."

"What about you?" David turned to me. "You climb?"

Alex caught my attention before I could answer. His eyes implored me to agree. I guess if two climbing buddies get hurt, it's better to have a third to call in the cavalry. I grinned.

"All the time."

CHAPTER TWENTY-TWO

David's truck smelled of woodchips and motor oil. Alex sat between us, and the vinyl seat groaned every time someone moved. He'd loaned Alex and me some rustic clothing and a couple pairs of old hiking boots. "Weathered," as he'd described them, "but they'll do the trick." I tightened the laces on mine to cinch down the large shoe size.

Our destination was the Inyo National Forest. To my surprise, David eagerly lectured on local history, informing us that "Inyo" is a Paiute Indian word meaning "dwelling place of a great spirit." Maybe he felt pressured to talk in such confined quarters. Alex responded well to the area's Native American routes, offering what he knew of the Suquamish and a few other Seattle tribes. LA's ancestry was generally unknown to me—except I'd once heard the Cahuenga Pass was originally an Indian burial ground. That tidbit cropped up every time I sat in bumper-to-bumper traffic on the Hollywood Freeway. I'd always considered that canyon to be cursed, even before I learned of the possible reason why.

I could see Mount Whitney through my window. As the highest peak in the neighboring forty-eight states, she carried a large tourist appeal. David had climbed the main path several times—of which he said the grade was level enough even for amateurs to scale—as well as an alternate, mountaineering route. Today, we headed toward a shorter summit in the shadow of Whitney where sightseers were guaranteed to be absent.

"Who taught you to climb?" Alex asked.

"No one. Learned by doing."

"What do you like about it?"

David shrugged. "Nature. Self-reliance. Solitude."

Farther up the road, the hill fell into a steep incline to our left and rose on our right. David certainly knew his way along this pass. I wondered how often he came out here, and whether he'd invited anyone to join him before. His chatty self fell quiet again. Anxiously tapping the steering wheel, he seemed intent on getting out of the car and onto the rock.

I kept an eye open for a parking lot. Instead, David pulled over in an ordinary turnout and ground the shifter into park.

"We're here," he said.

Alex looked out the window. "Where's the trailhead?"

"We make our own."

We each strapped on small daypacks complete with some energy bars, flashlights (even though we planned to finish before dark), windbreakers, and built-in water bladders with drinking hoses tied to our shoulders. Teeth marks had flattened my straw's mouthpiece. I moved it aside and followed David through a thick of trees. Fallen pine needles softened the ground. Our cushioned steps plodded over rocks and branches until the woods thinned out and the gritty soil surfaced. At the tree line stood a vertical sheet of stone. I had no idea how he expected us to climb that.

"This way," David said.

He walked alongside the mountain for twenty yards before he disappeared behind the rock face. The magic trick piqued Alex's curiosity. He quickened his pace to discover where his dad had gone.

As it turned out, the granite's curve hid an opening, like a narrow doorway, that exposed the start of a rough trail. Alex flicked his eyebrows at me, amused with the excursion.

"Happy to be out of your cubicle?" he asked.

"You have no idea."

We weaved around a footpath. My eye only saw the route's next part after each step. Looking ahead, I would have never considered navigating this groove had David not already forged through. He maintained a generous lead. Now knowing the course was possible, the path became a puzzle that begged a solution.

He didn't offer guidance on our ascent. We were more climbing acquaintances than teammates, but he did check on us occasionally. After he confirmed we hadn't tumbled to the ground, he pushed forward.

The path grew more challenging the higher we rose. Hiking turned to minimal scrambling. We grasped onto rocks and used our legs to push ourselves up to the next shelf. The incline David had considered "taking it easy" still required a decent amount of work. Alex advanced quicker than me. His claim to have climbing experience must have had some merit. That's when I felt a jagged chunk of rock bounce off my shoulder.

I looked up to see Alex's foothold had broken. His hand locked onto the ledge above as his feet kicked to find a new support.

"You okay up there?" I asked.

"Help."

David heard the commotion and looked down. I climbed higher since I was too far below to assist. I prayed Alex didn't slip since, among other reasons, he would fall right on top of me. David scuttled down and reached him first. He clamped his hand over Alex's to fortify his hold.

"Swing your foot to your left," he said. "See the thin channel there?"

Alex tapped his foot in the suggested direction. The tip of his boot scraped against the cliff, searching for the groove he couldn't find. I hardly saw it even with my better vantage.

"You're right on it," David said.

"I can't feel it."

"Just put your weight down. Trust me."

Alex obeyed. His struggling stopped. His toe balanced precariously on the minimal foothold.

"Now push yourself up."

Alex's free hand reached the next rock. He rose to a larger plateau, where he was able to rest for a moment. I caught up a minute later.

"You okay?" I asked.

David continued upward while Alex took a few moments to catch his breath. Despite his fright or fatigue, his smile told me he still enjoyed himself. Then, he continued on.

I took a moment to look across the treetops from

our new height. Shannon will never believe I did this. I snapped a couple photos with my phone as proof, then looked straight down to see how far we'd climbed. I'd never been good at estimating heights, but the distance was great enough to convince me to keep my eyes skyward. I refocused on the task at hand. Fortunately, my learning curve also distracted me. I was improving as a mountaineer. I closed on Alex's lead. Before I knew it, I was right on his tail. That's when I realized my climbing hadn't necessarily sped up; Alex's ascent had slowed.

He breathed heavily.

"What's up, buddy?" I asked.

His inhalations became shallow. "I don't feel so good."

"Just rest right there. You're in a good position. David!"

David looked down again. His reaction seemed a curious mixture of concern and annoyance. He moved down anyway.

"You said you've climbed before," he said.

"I have," Alex said. "I guess, maybe, I haven't been this high."

"Altitude sickness." He frowned at the verdict.

"Is he going to be all right?" I asked.

"He's probably used to hiking in Seattle just above sea level. We began at 9000 feet. It's a big difference."

"How can we help?" I asked.

"We have to descend. Did you hear that, Alex?"

More rapid breaths. "I'm tired."

"I know you are," David said, "but we're going to guide you down. We'll take it slow."

David glanced at the peak he wouldn't reach today.

He lowered himself to Alex's side and coached his son down rock by rock. He also advised him to periodically take small sips of water to remain hydrated. I drank from my chewed mouthpiece, too, just in case. I helped guide his feet when necessary.

Soon enough, a cold wind arrived. Stopping for the day sounded more appealing the quicker the temperature dropped.

CHAPTER TWENTY-THREE

On the trek back to the car, David didn't respond to any of our questions with more than two-word answers, save for the confirmation, "Alex will be fine." Nothing was spoken on the drive down the mountain.

Back at his house I thanked him and said, "We'll see you later." David grunted. He pulled himself onto the skeletal frame of his future sunroom, strapped on his tool belt, and went to work.

Alex looked exhausted.

"How you feeling?" I asked.

"Still have a headache, but at least the world stopped spinning."

I was sore and dirty. I must have been tired because normally I would have taken the time to clean off rather than soil my Mustang's interior. The car was due for detailing after this trip anyway.

"How you doing with everything else?" I asked.

His neck rolled against the headrest to face me. He scrutinized my face to see what I really meant.

Then my phone rang. He cringed at the sound.

"Sorry." I flipped open the handset. "Hello?"

"What are you kids up to?" Jacqueline asked.

She and I had spoken more this week than we had in years.

"Just finished a bit of mountain climbing," I said.

"I didn't figure you for the outdoors type."

"Just going with the flow. Can I call you later?"

"Let's grab some dinner."

I huffed in exasperation. "I told you: we're in Lone Pine."

She laughed.

"So am I, silly. I'm staying at the Best Western."

"You're what?"

"Decided to get out of LA. Was bored. Wanted to hang with you guys. Check out a new city—well, town. Take your pick. This place is so freaking small."

I was too tired to press her further as to why she drove all the way out here on a whim. Then again, she's done crazier things before. Maybe her arrival was just what we needed. Jacqueline could be counted on for a good time. I also worried she might remind Alex too much of Seattle. Either way, I had to try something new.

She definitely had too much free time on her hands.

CHAPTER TWENTY-FOUR

J acqueline leaned against the doorjamb of her motel room. The ceiling light highlighted traces of red in her chestnut-colored hair, still wet from a recent shower. She wore a red blouse with its wide collar delicately balanced on both shoulders. The shirt's loose fit still couldn't hide the curves beneath.

"Evening, boys. You look like hell."

"Long day," I said.

She looked us over. "You want something clean to wear?"

Alex shrugged.

"Come on." She grabbed his hand and pulled him past the beds with knotted pine headboards and floral comforters. She flipped open her suitcase and flung a male dress shirt at Alex. "Here. You look good in white."

He fingered the shirt's collar.

"Would you mind if I took a quick shower?" he asked. "I don't think a new shirt's going to do the trick."

"Go for it."

Her pinkie scratched his shoulder as he passed. He closed the bathroom door and switched on the water as

I got hit in the face with a shirt of my own. Jacqueline laughed. "And one for you."

I expected her to turn around or fiddle with the TV's remote to give me some privacy. She didn't. I unbuttoned my shirt and slid it off my shoulders. She'd thrown me a nice Perry Ellis—blue with white pinstripes. The feeling of fresh cotton felt soothing over my skin.

"You carry around guys' shirts just in case?"

"I like to sleep in them," she said.

Fastening the final button, I crossed to a guitar leaning against the wall. I picked up the acoustic by its neck and sat on the edge of the bed. The wood felt comforting. My fingers ran along the soundboard, between the steel strings, over the frets. I strummed an awful G chord before grabbing the strings to stop the vibrations.

"I didn't know you played," I said. "It's out of tune, though."

She glided across the carpet, her jeans scrunching around her bare feet. She sighed with pleasured exhaustion as her hips slinked onto the mattress beside me.

"I don't," she said. "Well, not yet anyway. I'm trying to learn." She took the guitar and rested it on her knee, as though readying a song. "It's my ex's. Mostly I like the way it looks in my apartment."

"How you doing with that?"

"Eric?"

I nodded.

"Better now that he broke up with that girl."

I turned in surprise. "Ashley tell you that?"

"She tried to be discrete about it. She still doesn't

know I know."

"I thought you two weren't friends."

"We still talk occasionally. Wait. How'd you know it was her?"

"We ran into them at Brian and Meghan's."

"Really?" she said with more curiosity than I'd expected. "Alex must have loved that."

"Highlight of the evening."

She plucked a simple scale. In the bathroom, the shower stopped. She tilted her head that direction. "He all right?"

I'd been undecided the whole ride over whether to tell her about the circumstances of our trip. She'd be a valuable ally, but I didn't know if she would come on too strongly. She might be an even better collaborator if she didn't know the particulars of our deadline.

"Anything you can do to help him figure out he doesn't need Ashley would be appreciated."

"Of course," she said.

I took back the instrument. The guitar sang a familiar bluesy tune I hadn't heard in years but easily returned to me.

"What song is that?"

"I don't know what it's called. It's something I made up a long time ago."

I fumbled the chord and clamped down on the neck.

"What's wrong?" she asked.

Something. A thought. I didn't know what. My nail scratched the metal string as I tried to chase it down. The friction made a horrid noise I couldn't force myself to stop. Jacqueline touched her fingers to mine, bringing me back to the present.

"The one person you can never get away from is yourself," I said. "But what if you hate yourself?"

"You're not planning on offing yourself, are you?"

I smiled. "No."

"Good. Because you would've picked a random person to come out to."

"Hypothetically speaking. I don't know. Maybe it's not even hate. Maybe it's just frustration. Or boredom. When life becomes a chore. Have you ever had to deal with that?"

She seemed engaged. Whether she accepted the discussion as theoretical or knew my words carried more weight, she didn't let on.

"It's part of the game," she said. "But you charge ahead anyway. Makes us appreciate the good times."

She gave my hand a look of concern, as if my nail was about to scratch the string again. I handed her back the guitar. She swiveled around the corner of the bed to lean the instrument against the nightstand.

"What brought all this on?" she asked.

"Nothing. It's just... Do you ever wish you could make someone do something? Just say, 'Hey, this is how it is. Deal with it.'"

She stretched her arms to either side, pulling the shirt tight against her chest. "All the time."

Alex returned from the bathroom looking rejuvenated.

"Your turn for a shower?" she asked me.

"I'm good." I stood up. "But if you'll excuse me for a moment..."

Alex took my seat on the bed, and she twisted to face him. I flicked on the bathroom light and shut the door.

After I washed my face, I pressed my palms against the cool, porcelain vanity. My tired reflection looked back at me, water dripping from his chin. I half-expected him to say something. I shook my head to ward off the encroaching desire for sleep.

I reached for a towel when I heard the delicate *clink* of glass. I must have kicked something, so I searched the floor for the object.

At the base of the toilet rested a vial the size of a peanut. I picked it up. Held it against the light. Salt-like grains fell toward the plastic cap.

For some reason I'd expected a pill, but that form was probably reserved for government spies and noir films—not the general public. Alex wasn't joking after all. The container must have fallen out of his jeans when he took the shower. The amount was just enough to stir into a glass of water to give you a headache you wouldn't wake from.

But what if it was just salt? A bluff.

I unscrewed the top, nervously brought the vile under my nose. I sniffed as quickly as I moved the substance away. The contents faintly smelled of almonds, but not the kind I would want to eat. For sure, something toxic.

Laughter filtered from the room. I screwed the cap back on and hid the cyanide in my pocket.

CHAPTER TWENTY-FIVE

After a steak dinner at Margie's Merry-Go-Round, Jacqueline drove us on a secret field trip in her black Jeep Wrangler. Lone Pine's closed storefronts and houses peered through gently lit windows. Alex probably thought the town looked restful. I felt it was lying in wait. Another block later, the settlement fell behind and the desert took over.

She and Alex exchanged occasional glances, simply enjoying each other's company. He liked it when she scratched the top of his back as a tactile hello.

Several turns later, the road eventually dead-ended into several lines of parked cars. This was the largest gathering we'd seen since our arrival here—oddly enough without any drivers in sight. Most of the license plates hailed from California, but I saw a couple Nevadas, an Arizona, and a random Georgia peach. Jacqueline found an open spot and added the token Washington vehicle to the mix.

"Come on," she said.

Alex followed without question. I went along out of curiosity. A chain-link gate blocked off what must have been a state park. The sign to the left read: TRAILS CLOSED AFTER SUNSET. We hopped the fence and followed her down the wooded path. Alex powered ahead with an excited grin plastered over his face. After a few steps, he put his hands in his pockets. His eyes shot open in surprise. His hands sifted around and dug deeper. Not finding what he wanted, he searched the ground where he'd jumped the fence.

My fingers pinched the vial in my own pocket. If I let go for even a moment, I feared my leverage would disappear.

"What's wrong?" I asked.

He stopped searching. "Nothing." He continued after Jacqueline.

My thumb made sure the cap stayed tight. I pulled out the vile and flung it in the bushes.

"By the way," she said, "watch out for rattlesnakes."

I quickly looked around to make sure I hadn't aggravated one by littering. I began to question this off-road expedition, especially after my healthy of dose of nature earlier today.

"Are you able to navigate in the dark?" I asked.

She grunted. "You don't grow up in Seattle without learning your way through the woods at night."

I'd only seen her wear nicer clothing. Even though she was dressed more casually now, her shirt and jeans were designer. I tried picturing her hiking once upon a time wearing the Rainy City uniform of boots, fleece, and one of those knitted hats with earflaps and tassels. The image eluded me. I'd once asked Alex why so many people dressed that way. I joked about the ensemble's lack of fashion. He defended its comfort.

As it turned out, we didn't need a flashlight. The

moon brightened the path ahead. The amber eyes of a deer glowed from the underbrush to my right. Once the animal determined we weren't a threat, it dipped its head down to continue eating the white flowers off a bush.

"So, Alex," Jacqueline began, "how've you been?"

She gave me a wink to let me know she was helping out. That single bat of her eyelid eased some of the load from my shoulders.

"Fine," he lied, wiping the sweat from his forehead with the back of his hand. He frantically searched me with his eyes. "Did you take it?"

"Take what?"

He didn't believe me and put some distance between us.

"It's okay if you're not," she said. "It's been a crazy few weeks."

"Tell us what we can do to help," I added.

His distress grew.

"Not everything has a simple answer, Ed."

"He knows that," she said as she ducked under a low branch. "Everyone goes through rough patches. Look at Ed and Shannon."

"Yes, Shannon. There's a success story for ya."

The unexpected sarcasm stopped me in my tracks. There was no need to take shots at her. Even Jacqueline knew that.

"Take it easy," she said.

Alex turned to face me. "You want to know why Shannon's so upset with you?"

"Because I haven't proposed to her."

"No. You're resting on your laurels."

"My what?"

"You figure she'll always be there, which means you can put off making a decision. So when she leaves, you'll have no right to complain."

I felt my face flush, but all I could do was say, "Like Ashley, right?"

He took the blow in stride.

Jacqueline stepped between us. "How about we just cool it, guys?"

"Neither of you communicate," I went on. "I know she's incapable of telling you this, but have you ever considered she was happy about losing the baby because you two weren't ready?"

"Ashley had a miscarriage?" Jacqueline said.

Alex rolled his eyes, displeased that I'd leaked that information. "I drove her away. I know that."

"That's not what I'm saying." I tried to think of a way to clarify my point. "Remember when you two were dating, and she blamed you for not spending enough time with her? Then she said you were never apart. She has no clue what she wants."

His brow wrinkled. "She's gotten better with that. I was willing to put in the time to help her out. It's called commitment."

"Alex, nothing's good enough for her. If she makes you think it's your fault, then it takes the heat off her. It looks like confidence, but it's cowardice."

He lunged past Jacqueline, grabbed my shirt, and shoved me with his fists. My heels struck an exposed tree root, and I hit the ground with a thud. He restrained himself from unleashing a slew of accusations and, rather, deliberately said, "Don't ever talk about her that way."

I slowly rose to my feet. Jacqueline remained a safe

distance behind him.

"I'll take the hit on that one," I said. "I'm sorry to tell you this, but if Ashley cared about you as much as you thought, she'd return your calls."

No sooner had I finished my sentence, his phone rang. He pulled the black device from his pocket. The number shocked him at first; then it brought on a triumphant smile. He showed me the screen as evidence of his victory. "Ashley Calling." He walked off to hold their discussion in private.

I plopped back on the ground, and Jacqueline sat beside me. I arched my back to shake off the lingering discomfort as I looked around, trying to find the source a resonant sound nearby. I could've sworn I heard drums.

"What are the odds that she'd call right then?" I said.

Jacqueline picked at something beneath her nail. "No odds. I told her to call tonight after I tracked you two down."

She interpreted my surprise as an accusation.

"What?" she said. "I got them to talk. Sue me."

"You're here on Ashley's behalf?"

"I'm here for myself. She just happened to call when I was driving. I picked up the phone thinking it was Alex. Their names look similar at a glance."

"Ashley and Alex," I mused.

"It's sickening how cute it sounds."

He paced the dirt in the distance, too far to be within earshot.

"If it helps," she continued, "I think you made a good point earlier."

"Thanks. It doesn't."

After his feet carved a circle in the ground, Alex finished the call and returned.

"So?" Jacqueline said.

He swung his phone back and forth between his fingers.

"Well," he began, "she was very apologetic, again with, 'It's not what you think, it's not what you think.' I said, 'Forgive me, but I'm a little surprised you're so concerned all of a sudden.' She said she's always cared and nothing happened with Eric."

He scoffed. I was unsure whether he believed her.

"He was back in town," Alex continued, "wanted to talk, wanted her back. She got confused because—that's right, Ed—she and I weren't communicating. God, I hate that guy," he said under his breath. "He was her first 'real' love, so she'll always care about him on some level. But high school's over and she loved me, blah blah blah."

"She loves you," I said. "That's not blah. That's huge."

He dismissed my comment with a wave of his hand.

"She wanted to know if I'll be back for the wedding. I told her I didn't know and I'd talk to her later."

"That's it?" Jacqueline asked.

He smiled. "That's it."

"And you believed her about Eric?" she said.

"She sounded sincere enough." He stopped playing with the phone and slipped it back in his pocket. "I don't know. Maybe I should be alone for a while. She wanted time off, so her wish is my command."

"Nothing quite like an ego boost," Jacqueline said. "Come on. I have something to show you."

She stood and led us through the shrubbery.

"She must have said something else," I said to Alex.

"That's it." He was more interested in Jacqueline's surprise than answering my questions.

Now I wondered if I'd been mistaken. When we ran into Ashley at Brian's place a few days ago, maybe Eric's hand on her hip was an unwelcomed advance rather than an approved sign of affection. Maybe she threw off his grip so Alex wouldn't get the wrong idea, and her apologetic look was genuine concern rather than guilt. That would explain the tearful phone call we heard on the drive home. Then again, her new story could be a justified lie, a dishonesty to spare Alex the pain. I didn't know anymore. I looked heavenward as if maybe the answer would reveal itself to me.

No dice.

Instead, the open sky burned with countless stars. Such a natural sight amazed Angelenos for these nighttime pinpricks were an uncommon treat back home.

Then there was that sound again.

The drums.

Light began to flicker on the other side of the trees. We came to the edge of the woods, where the dirt hill sunk into a sprawling crater, and from its heart, rose a massive bonfire.

Leave it to Jacqueline to find something like this. I swore she lived in a different world than everyone else.

Alex strode past me in a trance, drawn to the heat and the shadows dancing around the flames to a multitude of percussion. We made our way down the hill. Alex and Jacqueline began jogging. I walked.

The kettledrums intensified. The band stretched

across two tiers carved into the crater's walls. I couldn't see them as much as their hands. A trumpet and trombone joined the tribal chorus. There were bongos. Djembes. Talking drums. A didgeridoo. Primal sounds. The closer I walked the music was not so much heard as felt.

Random groups of people danced around the fire. Kids with their college sweatshirts. Surfers far from the beach. Hackie sackers and mountain climbers. A bare-chested man wearing fur pants and Viking horns swung chains attached to fist-sized globes of fire. The flashing of light and shadows accentuated the muscles of his arms, the ripples of his stomach.

Across the flames, a woman in a fur skirt and leather bodice twirled fire batons. She dug her bare feet into the soft earth. She arched her back and bounced her shoulders to the beat of the drums.

Mobs leapt and danced around me. Everyone had stopped thinking. They only moved. I wondered how many knew what was actually going on. Or how many people joined by coincidence like Alex and me.

He and Jacqueline danced around the blaze. They'd surrendered themselves to the mood like everyone else. Her clothes clung to his body, and Alex's sweaty face reflected the orange light. She wrapped her arm around him. He closed his eyes and smiled bigger than I'd ever seen.

I considered leaving him with his celebration. I wanted to quit because he was right. How could I convince him to forget Seattle when I wasn't any better? I was just as bad as Ashley. As Brian. I was driving Shannon away. I didn't know what was going on anymore. Or who I was. Meanwhile, Alex continued to dance. He was enjoying life.

Seeing him now, maybe I had done my job, even if it didn't turn out exactly the way I'd planned. By morning, he'll be fine. He seemed so positive after speaking with his wife. On the other hand, that was the way he'd confessed his suicide plan, too.

I needed to find out where he stood, whether he moved in a new direction or if this carnival was just another part of his last hurrah. Ashley had taken off, along with Brian and Meghan, leaving him stranded like a blushing memory to their backs. I didn't want to be them, but at the same time, I was losing my grip.

CHAPTER TWENTY-SIX

The bonfire high continued on the ride home. Jacqueline had brought four bottles of wine from LA. Alex was into the idea, and I could use a drink. I grabbed the first bottle from the cargo space and passed it forward. He opened the Cabernet with the waiter's corkscrew that lived in the glove compartment.

I carried the remaining bottles into her motel room. She pulled her golden pillbox from her jeans and offered me a Vicodin. I declined. She held up the pill to Alex.

"Already got one from the bathroom."

"Time to celebrate," she said, swallowing the tablet, "now that you don't want Ashley back."

He cheered, throwing his fist in the air like a sports fan. My mood lightened the more I drank.

She made another trip to her car and returned with sourdough pretzels, seedless grapes, and turkey and cheddar Lunchables. The girl knew how to travel. Already a wine bottle down, the food selection thrilled Alex. He launched into a tirade about the significance Oscar Mayer Lunchables held when we were kids, how they were the cool things to eat and homemade sandwiches just didn't cut it. Jacqueline laughed at his antics and playfully smacked his shoulder.

The next bottle of Pinot had clearly put to bed his remaining inhibitions. Everything was twisted into a sexual innuendo. Slurred speech was the epitome of hilarity, which was even more comical because we knew that wouldn't be the case any other time than tonight. Alex's enjoyment translated into mine. I never realized how much I missed his laugh.

Still, despite my amusement, I knew I would enjoy the evening even more if Shannon were here.

We had teetered over the edge of inebriation when Jacqueline said, "I hate to keep bringing her up, but I think you're better off without Ash."

He drove the suggestion around the block a few times.

"I know you have to say that," he said.

"I don't have to say anything." She laid her hand on his knee. "Believe me. She's never known a good thing when she has it."

He placed his hand on top of hers, and she laced her French-tipped nails through his fingers. She gave him a squeeze, then turned to me.

"How you feeling, Eddie?"

I was feeling the wine. I stood from the desk chair and made my way across the room. "I'll be right back." I accidentally kicked the luggage next to the TV and almost fell. "Easy, tiger," Alex said. I waved to let them know I'd be all right.

She moved closer to him. As I closed the front

door behind me, I heard her begin to say, "You want to know a secret?"

The Best Western Frontier Motel was shaped like a horseshoe. The various rooms wrapped around three sides of a gated swimming pool and pool house adorned with wagon wheels. I couldn't decide whether the air brushing through the parking lot was hot or cold. I walked from the doorway and dialed my phone. The rings repeated while I pretended the sidewalk's curb was a tightrope.

"Hello?"

I'd always loved the calm of Shannon's voice when she woke in the morning.

"Sorry," I said. "I took a chance you were up."

"It's fine. I haven't really been able to sleep."

I paced the walkway in front of Jacqueline's door.

"You know what I do when that happens?" I said. "Math. By the time I try to divide 190,032 by 107, I'm so bored I'm out."

"Have you been drinking?"

I stepped on my foot while crossing over in place. "A little. But that's not why I'm calling."

"Why then?"

I breathed deeply. "I didn't mean to blow you off earlier. Alex really needed me this week, and I couldn't let him go alone."

"Why didn't you just say that?"

Good question. She made it sound like that was the most obvious and forgivable explanation.

"I don't know," I said.

A heavyset man exited the motel lobby. It was

comforting to know someone else was up at this hour. His keys echoed across the courtyard. Through the shadows, I could make out his plaid flannel shirt. The people around here sure liked flannel.

I said, "I wanted to be more specific with you. Like—" I couldn't hear her on the other line anymore. "Shannon? Hello?"

"Like what?"

The man's footsteps continued toward his car. I waited for his door to close, so he didn't overhear my conversation. He started his engine and drove away.

"Like what?" she said again.

"I don't know. There's so much to say. I'll tell you all about it when I get home."

"I take it you won't be back in the morning."

"No. Why?"

She sighed.

"I'm leaving for Baltimore tomorrow afternoon."

"So soon?"

"I told you. I can't pass up this opportunity. I start Monday."

"Wait for me," I said. "I'm coming back."

"My flight's at 4:30."

"We'll talk about this."

"I have to finish packing."

"Just wait for me," I said.

Her demeanor was calm. I'd always admired her ability to make decisions, which usually were the right ones. This time her resolve was not in my favor.

"I've waited long enough," she said. "Call me tomorrow."

She hung up.

My phone slapping shut had to be the only sound

for miles. The night air was definitely cold.

All my life I've never known how a woman could close the door so soundly once she's made up her mind when a man could never hope for such clarity. Shannon was doing to me what Ashley did to Alex. Both girls committed to a decision and followed through, and like him, my hands were tied, unable to prevent what'll happen next.

But Shannon wasn't Ashley. I wasn't going to let that happen to me. Our conversation sobered me to the point where I felt I hadn't touched a drink all night. I had to tell Alex we needed to go home. We still had two days left in our bargain, but Shannon was leaving in one.

I stepped off the curb with ease.

As I opened the motel door, I found Alex and Jacqueline kissing. He leaned over her, his hand touching her bare shoulder where her shirt collar had slid off.

She pulled him closer, but he jumped backward. She left her collar where it lay and sat up against the headboard.

"Oh, come on," she said. "You're not going to have a little fun after what she's done to you? I thought you didn't want her anymore."

"I don't know," he said.

"You don't owe anybody anything. If you're not going to look out for yourself, who will? Am I right, Ed?"

Both turned to me as if I was supposed to cast the tie-breaking vote. She made a good point. This was his time.

"She's right," I said. She grinned at Alex. I kept my

eye on her. "But it looks like he doesn't agree with your agenda."

She pulled her collar back onto her shoulder. "I thought we were a team, Eddie."

Alex stuttered. "Ashley said she didn't cheat."

"Who cares if she did or didn't?" Jacqueline stood up, perfectly poised. "She left you. That's what counts."

He looked confused and disgusted—with Jacqueline, with himself. He turned on his heel, slammed into my shoulder, and continued out the door. I called after him, but he didn't stop.

I waited for Jacqueline to say something. She removed a compact from the suitcase's outer pocket, flipped the mirror open, checked her lipstick, fixed her hair. When she was satisfied, she looked up.

"What happened?" I asked.

Her eyes said everything with their emptiness.

"*C'est la vie.*"

CHAPTER TWENTY-SEVEN

Alex passed the motel's closed doors and darkened windows. He locked his attention straight ahead. I jogged to catch up. His speed quickened with mine. As soon as he reached the end of the parking lot, he bolted down the highway.

I ran after him. His feet slammed into the pavement quicker and harder than mine. The faster I ran to catch him, the farther he led. Alex kept going until he slipped on a patch of gravel. He hit the ground, giving me enough time to catch up. When he tried to stand, I pushed him down. He rolled into a sitting position, his hands angled behind him in support.

His eyes were bloodshot. He tried to calm himself but wasn't succeeding.

"Breathe," I said.

Except for the faint glow of the motel lights far behind us, we were alone among a row of storefronts resembling lifeless movie facades. The atmosphere was balmier out here. His hyperventilating began to slow. Every sound faded into the darkness.

"She said she's always liked me."

"Who?" I asked.

"Jacqueline. She kissed me. I said this wasn't right. She tried to convince me. Said it would make Eric and Ashley jealous."

"There's nothing to worry about."

"I told her I wouldn't do it just for that. She said to do it for myself."

He staggered to his feet. He swayed a bit from either the alcohol or the Vicodin. Probably both.

"It wasn't you," I said. "It was her."

"They wanted me to move up there with them."

"Come on. Let's get the car."

"I was going to open a studio. Teach art at Brian's family's camp. Ashley and I were going to raise our kids in our house. It's nice. You've seen it."

"It is."

"Buy a boat. Play baseball. They— They promised. I— I can't breathe." He drew short breaths at a rapid pace. He grabbed his chest. "It hurts."

"Try to relax."

"It burns. I can't— I can't do this."

I moved closer to lend support, but he pushed me away. I stepped toward him again. He shoved harder. I grabbed his wrist. He tried to break away, resisting with what little energy and will remained. I embraced him. His squirming faded into acceptance, and finally, when he could no longer fight, he hugged me back.

FRIDAY

CHAPTER TWENTY-EIGHT

Alex didn't so much fall asleep as pass out. I propped myself against the headboard to stay awake and keep an eye on him. First I tried to work on my laptop, but alcohol and an already long day didn't lend well to accurate work.

The previous night's chase down Main Street played on a loop in my head. The scenarios of "what if he hadn't tripped?" and "what if I hadn't caught him?" filtered through my tangle of thoughts. He ran as though he'd taken flight, trying to catch the evening stars while I desperately reached for his foot before he ignited like a mass of flares and candlewicks. That was the extent of his determination. His artistic temperament underwent higher highs and lower lows than most people could appreciate. While it was easy for me to wonder about his passion and his heightened, synesthetic experiences, I often ignored the flip side.

I dozed off a couple times during my watch. When I awoke, to my relief, he hadn't budged. At one point

I checked his phone to put to rest a lingering doubt. Jacqueline had told the truth that Ashley, Brian, and Meghan had been trying to reach him. He'd missed calls from all three.

I checked my phone for voicemails. None. Why hadn't they called me? I checked my e-mail in case they tried to reach me there. Indeed, a message had been waiting for a couple days:

Ed,

No one seems to have your phone number. I don't know if you've changed it since college. I feel weird that this is the first thing I write you in a while since we haven't really kept in touch, but that's a discussion for another time.

I need to know if Alex is with you. He's not returning any of my calls, and I'm worried. Let me know he's okay. He's never taken off like this before. Please have him call me.

Tell him I'm sorry.

Ashley

The sky eventually turned a hazy blue, and my hunger returned. Alex awoke two hours later. He rubbed his eyes to focus on me watching from the chair.

"Ashley e-mailed me," I said.

He stood and stretched. Walked to the bathroom. "I don't want to talk about it."

The door clicked shut.

We spent the morning on a hillside road overlooking the town we'd grown accustomed to the past several days. We sat on the front end of my car drinking orange juice and eating doughnuts: ideal hangover food.

Down below, a couple trucks swept the streets like ants in a maze. The locals went about their daily lives. No one knew we were up here. Our impact had been minimal. To the motel clerk and diner staff, we were just travelers passing through, sure to be forgotten as soon as we leave.

Alex stared ahead. He held a secret deliberation while grinding his jaw. I used the downtime to recharge and finish my doughnut. I crumbled my napkin, shoved it through the OJ carton's triangular mouth. I offered to take his trash. He looked at me for the first time in a half hour.

"Come on," he said.

David's front door was open. Just inside, a giant duffle lay on the tile. Kiana barked and ran down the stairs to greet us. She'd taken well to Alex. He stroked her back as she rubbed her side against his knees.

"Okay, girl," David said, pounding down the stairs. "I'll feed you, I'll feed you." He saw us and slowed on the last two steps before he recomposed himself. "Haven't had enough yet?"

"We came to return the hiking gear you lent us," Alex said.

He nodded. "Put it there."

I set the boots and folded clothes next to the luggage.

"Where you off to?" Alex asked.

He didn't answer. He made his way to the kitchen instead. "Come on, Kiana." She ran after him. We followed, too.

From a Tupperware bin he scooped two helpings of dog food with an old, enamel-coated coffee mug. Kiana dove head first into her bowl.

"What's going on?" Alex said.

David loaded the dishwasher. "I have some things to take care of out of town."

"Nothing serious, I hope."

"No," he said, still loading. "Just have to go away for a few days."

"Okay. We'll be heading back to Seattle soon," Alex began. "So how about I call you when you get back? There's still so much I want to learn about Annie. My medical history. About you."

Shoving a plate into the dishwasher, he said under his breath, "What did I get myself into?"

I wasn't sure whether I'd heard him correctly, but the confused looks Alex and I exchanged verified we'd likely heard the same response.

"What was that?" I asked.

David stopped cleaning. "I can't do this anymore." He turned toward us but kept his head down.

"There's no rush," Alex said.

"No," he said. He paused to collect his thoughts. "There's just no place for you in my life."

His words struck Alex like a punch to the gut.

"Why? Do I remind you too much of her or something?"

David rolled his eyes.

"You want to know about your mom? Fine. My brother planned to propose to her, but they had a fight. She and I got drunk. That's how you came to be. For your benefit, we tried to make it work, but that plan was obviously doomed from the start. And that's all I'm going to say." He looked straight into his son's eyes. "You both remind me of my big mistake."

We showed ourselves out.

CHAPTER TWENTY-NINE

I packed my bags at the motel. I removed my clothes from the drawers and stuffed the dirty laundry into plastic bags, including the shirt Jacqueline loaned me.

"You should be proud of what you did," I said, speaking loud enough for him to hear me. He'd been in the bathroom for a while with the door closed. "No one can blame you for trying." I paused between each of my points so he could let them sink in. "It's for the best. It may not seem like it for a while, but we came all the way out here and now we know, right?"

Still no response.

"This is good timing, too. I might be able to catch Shannon before her flight."

I'd also fallen behind on my work. I didn't want to mention how I needed to get back to the office to play catch up since he might take that as a rebuke of our entire trip. I looked around the room to make sure I hadn't missed anything. Other than my jacket hung over the chair, I was good to go.

He had yet to pack. A gentle prod was in order.

"What do you say, Alex? Let's get this show on the

road."

Still nothing.

"Alex?"

I opened the bathroom door, knocking as I went. I found him standing over the counter, razor blade to his wrist.

"What are you doing?" I said.

My voice startled him. He fumbled the razor into the sink. It bounced around the rim. I grabbed his hands to keep him from chasing the blade long enough for the metal to slip down the drain.

He released a guttural yell while shaking off my grip.

My adrenaline was pumping.

"You gave me a week," I said. "You're a day early. You broke your promise."

There was blood on my palms. I pulled his forearms toward me. He had a superficial cut across the scar tissue on his right wrist. His leather wristband lay unbuckled on the countertop. I dropped his hands and wiped mine clean with a towel. My face flushed so quickly it hurt.

"I know you think by killing yourself you're getting even with all of us. Yeah, we'd grieve, but we'd move on. Ashley will move on. Come to think of it: I doubt Brian would even give a shit."

"He will," Alex said.

"He might make an appearance at your funeral if he could fit it into his schedule. He'd give his condolences to Ashley. To me. Then he'll go back to merry ol' Seattle to live his perfect life with his perfect wife without a second thought about you. Sure, maybe someday he'll mention a friend he once knew from college who killed himself to make conversation at a dinner party. Then he'll move onto the next, cheerier subject.

"Oh. Speaking of positive notes, you were right last night. I did find your cyanide. I tossed it."

Alex finally learned where his ticket to the other side had gone. He looked as though he had turned from suicidal to homicidal.

"Why do you want to be like them anyway?" I continued. "They're boring. They go out to dinner, see a movie, then they go home and watch TV. It's always the same. Brian doesn't even venture from his standard catch phrases. That preppy, 'Heeyy, that was great,' and, 'Boy, I don't know.' He and Ashley even share the same jokes that were only funny the first fifteen times.

"And Ashley. Yeah. She'll remarry some sap who won't make her happy. She'll blame him for all her shortcomings, but the main point is, she won't be with you.

"I'll hate you for it. I'd be sad you're gone, but I'll get over it, and all our good memories will just be soured by the last one. So go ahead. Do it. No one's watching."

I tried to walk out. My feet, however, stayed planted on the bathroom tile. My words, which were yet to be acknowledged, had beaten him less severely than I'd expected. He continued to stand before me—dejected but resilient.

"Look. I know you've had a shitty week. Your mom's dead. David's not the dad you hoped for. Jacqueline is selfish as sin. Who cares? You have a new family who's happy to know you simply exist. For the first time you have grandparents. You have John in San Francisco. I helped you find them. *I* did. And you're throwing this all in my face.

"You have options, and if you're not willing to see that, I—" I threw up my hands in surrender. "I can't do this anymore."

I clutched my jacket off the chair, made sure my keys were in my pocket. My hand grabbed the bathroom doorjamb before it would let me leave. My fingers shook from the pressure.

"By the way," I said. "Happy birthday."

CHAPTER THIRTY

I circled Lone Pine to blow off steam. I lapped the town twice, which didn't take long given its size. This also gave me a chance to reconsider my decision. The opportunity came and went. Instead, I had a new resolve.

When I found my way back onto Main Street, I continued forward. Fast. "Bat out of hell" didn't begin to describe how quickly I traveled. The devil would have to conjure some new creature to compete.

I passed a Highway Patrol cruiser at one point. I couldn't tell whether he was slowing down to ticket that red Jeep or speeding up to chase me. Either way, I never saw the cop again, and I didn't release the gas pedal until I arrived at LAX.

3:47 pm.

I parked on the departure level, then raced on foot across the bridge to terminal seven.

Shannon usually flew United. Since I was unable to reach her on her cell, I took a chance that she continued her habit. Inside, a mass of people and their matching luggage swarmed the check-in counters. More bodies were in this one terminal than the entire population of Lone Pine. I forced my way through a high school water polo team as well as a Korean tour group wearing neon yellow hats. I fought the sensory overload and searched head after head for auburn hair. Why couldn't she have been taller?

I looked for her bags. I ducked up and down as I continued on, hunting curls and a flowered suitcase. She always strapped a florescent green belt around the bag to make it easier to spot on the luggage carrousel. The same effect wasn't achieved here.

I yelled her name. The only responses were alternating inquisitive and angry stares. I cupped my hands around my mouth.

"Shannon!"

My cell phone had zero bars. Hers probably lacked reception, too. No wonder she didn't answer. I stepped up on the metal frame used to size carry-ons. I soon found the flimsy device wasn't designed to bear a person's weight, but I managed to keep my balance.

"Sir," the female attendant behind the counter said, "you're not supposed to be up there."

I scanned the terminal from my new vantage.

"Sir, you have to step down or I'll call security."

Thirty yards away, standing at an automated check-in screen, were auburn curls and a suitcase with a thick, green strap. She even wore her comfy LMU sweatshirt she loved to travel in—the one I'd bought her after she received her acceptance letter. An attendant exchanged her suitcase for a boarding pass. She headed in the opposite direction.

That's when a hand grabbed my arm. A security guard said, "Sir, please step down from there." I didn't know why I thanked him, but I did. Then I ran after her.

On the way I knocked a woman's bag off her shoulder. I apologized but kept moving. By the time I caught up, Shannon waited in line at the checkpoint. She showed her ID and boarding pass to the TSA officer, who waved her through. She placed her backpack and violin case on the X-ray conveyor belt.

"Shannon."

She turned to find me trapped on the other side of the crowd control stanchions. Her tired eyes took a moment to make sure they weren't hallucinating.

"Ed, what are you doing here?"

She stepped out of line to come to me. I tried to catch my breath.

"Don't go," I said.

"We've already discussed this."

"Not enough. I just drove two hundred miles so we could properly talk."

She looked both relieved and anxious. She glanced over her shoulder toward the metal detectors. The TSA officers with the blue latex gloves had selected her backpack for further inspection—probably since its owner was absent.

"I'm going to miss my flight."

I grabbed her hand.

"I'm here," I said. "Tell me what I can do to fix us."

"It doesn't work that way."

"Please. Don't go."

She stood up straight. I knew it didn't matter what I said. My mouth could spew promises to marry her and give her everything she wanted, even though I'd never make such deals just to make her stay. For some reason I maintained that absurd need to back up my words. Even if I said what she wanted to hear, and said it with utter honesty, she was getting on that plane.

"I can't do this now." She wrapped her arm around me and kissed my cheek. Her hair brushed my nose. It smelled of honeysuckle. "I'll arrange to get the rest of my stuff later. I also left the address of where I'll be staying on the kitchen counter. I hope to hear from you."

Then, she was gone.

CHAPTER THIRTY-ONE

I drove around for hours. Venice. Downtown. Hollywood. I finally made my way between the mountains, up the twisting 405 Freeway toward Mulholland. I was singing along to "Boys of Summer" on the radio at the top of my lungs, banging on the steering wheel to the beat. I wasn't the best singer, but I didn't care. My entire body moved with the pounding. My right hand flew in the air before slamming back into the leather-wrapped ring. Don Henley's lyrics thumped through my eardrums with newfound lucidity, and I scoffed at that last line of the verse.

Yeah, Don. If only I could let her go.

Pink and purple rays illuminated my fall down the other side of the mountain, into the valley, where the streetlights and house lights and store lights ignited one by one in all directions like a constellation of stars. They welcomed me into the new nightfall, the artificial astrology of urban life. I didn't know where I was heading. Control was overrated anyway. I'd let my whims take over for the first time, not caring if they guided me the long way to wherever.

I'd always liked the sound of "Ventura Boulevard." I exited there and rolled down the windows. My car drove east. A silver Charger and red Camaro raced down the opposite lane. On any other day I would have taken part in the fun.

I passed the '50s-themed Mel's Diner where some local band and their friends monopolized the front corner. They sat and stood in contorted positions and, as a whole, looked like an all-American Picasso painting. One guy with excessively tall spiked hair, a style only rock stars could get away with, sat atop the cream leather booth strumming his guitar. Girls adorned the bench around him. They gazed up with spangled eyes, and everyone animatedly sang along. This must have been a common occurrence since they had synchronized hand gestures already developed.

I'd only seen the group for a moment, but that was all the time I needed to secure the image. Years from now, I knew I'd be able to recall every detail. I wished I were in a band. That way all those people gazing at the guitarist would follow my lead.

I passed an old movie palace. Its heyday was long gone, and the sign told of its conversion into a Barnes and Noble. The marching marquee light bulbs reflected off my black hood as I waited for the stoplight to turn green. I watched the customers browse the seemingly endless shelves erected between the Art Deco flourishes of the forgotten theatre. A line stretched down the block for a book signing. The author greeted each enthusiast with a smile and a stroke of her pen.

I passed three or four Starbucks coffee houses on this street alone. After a while it's difficult to keep track of how many you come across in this town. Outside the last one, a brunette cheerleader with mysterious slits for eyes sat on her boyfriend's lap. He wrapped her in his coat to shield her from an unusually cold breeze. They took turns sipping a coffee. Their mouths breathed the steam of passion, the steam of candied caffeine, which was reinvigorated when their lips came together for a prolonged kiss. I couldn't tell whether she looked exactly like Shannon or completely different.

I still didn't know where I was headed. The car guided me onto familiar roads until the streets disappeared and the houses pulled back into the hills. I found myself staring at a red and white sign I knew well. "Home of the Cardinals."

Pine and eucalyptus trees surrounded the Westfield Academy baseball diamond, forging a sort of haven where the only sight was twilight overhead. I felt I was somewhere far away in the mountains, in another world entirely, forgetting that just past the trees and through the winding passageways of Coldwater Canyon lay metropolitan LA. This was a welcomed escape.

When I stepped onto the field for the first time in years, with that sharp smell of freshly cut grass still warm from the sun, I couldn't help but think of all those summer nights that used to drape me in nostalgia for an age so easily eluding my fingertips. I felt the familiar grind of infield dirt beneath my shoes. My head hung low to watch my feet balance along the first-base line, to see my toe drag across the chalk, creating a white crescent against the earth. I saw myself back when I used to play, fielding grounders at shortstop and throwing the ball to Alex at first. Those were our simple times. Some part of me still was that person, but the rest knew I could never be the same again. If only I could reach out and touch my former self.

I thought of all the players who must have rounded the bases on this very soil fifty years ago; how nothing else could have mattered than the crack of the bat, their teammates' cheers from the dugout, the smell of dirt woven in the seams of leather gloves. I could almost see those ballplayers, feel them, before they faded into the evening light, never to return except in memory.

No one knew I was here. Not even Shannon. What would she care anyway? I could've been driving off the edge of the Santa Monica Mountains and she wouldn't know the difference.

No.

I kicked the dirt at the idea. I kicked it again at the thought of her walking past airport security and onto the plane I couldn't follow. I'd taken the long road to return to where I'd begun when it was just me, whoever that was, when no one else told me who I was supposed to become. I'd returned to the place where I'd met Alex. Where I'd met her.

The girls' track team had been running laps on the other side of the outfield fence during our baseball practice. I saw her through the chain-link on my fourth time around the warning track. She was beautiful but in quiet way—that smooth skin and that auburn hair that bounced as she ran. I'd seen her around school and knew her name, but we hadn't spoken yet. We locked eyes as we paced each other. She gave a little smile the way you hoped a girl would when she liked you.

I slowed down on the next circuit. Coach McNabb didn't take long to notice. "Cohen," he yelled. "You love running laps so much, why don't you add another five?"

I found her behind the gym after practice. I learned

she played the violin, and I told her I sort of played the guitar.

"What kind of songs do you write?" she asked.

"Bad ones," I said.

Her dad picked her up that day, cutting our conversation short. When she drove off, I found McNabb chewing his sunflower seeds behind me.

"That the girl you were running with, Cohen?"

"Yeah, Coach."

"You get her number?"

She stole one last glance through the back window.

"She's playing hard to get," I said.

He spit shells onto the concrete. "Don't they all?"

My phone rang, shaking me back to the present. I wished I'd left it in the car. I glanced at the darkened track on the other side of the fence. Now, it didn't look the same.

I found the cell in my pocket. "Luis Calling." I flipped the handset open.

"You still sick?" he asked.

"Beyond sick."

"Good. There's a new club opening up tonight. You sound like you could use some fun."

I didn't know I sounded that bad. After he repeatedly begged for the cause of my exhaustion, I told him about Shannon.

"All the more reason, man. C'mon."

I no longer had any energy left to fight my coworker. Besides, where else would I go tonight?

CHAPTER THIRTY-TWO

L uis was a senior-level programmer in his early thirties. He dressed like a high roller and, with what he could afford, led the lifestyle to boot. The designer wardrobe and machismo attitude compensated for some latent insecurity I didn't care to uncover.

He picked me up at nine, to my surprise, with two girls in tow. This bad idea just got worse.

"Lindsay, Tanya, this is Ed." I wasn't sure which girl was which. It didn't matter anyway. The brunette sat shotgun. I hesitated before sliding into the backseat of his Jaguar next to the blond—possibly Lindsay.

"Nice to meet you," she said, leaning over to give me a peck on the cheek. A smile spread across Luis' face. I wondered what he'd told her about me. She looked too trendy for her own good: straight hair, dark eyeliner, and a wrap-over top with a plunging neckline that accentuated her breasts. Normally she would have been attractive if I didn't know thirty duplicates were sure to be at the club. Tanya was the brunette version.

The rap music blasting through the stereo denied any possibility of conversation. To be honest, I was glad. I wasn't in the mood for chitchat since Luis' erratic driving concerned me more. While I drove fast, I also drove straight.

Shannon texted me five blocks later. "Layover in Orlando." I couldn't imagine how she wanted me to respond.

"Who was that?" he asked.

"Your girlfriend?" Lindsay said.

"He doesn't have a girlfriend anymore." He winked at me in the rearview.

"It's complicated," I said.

"That's too bad." Lindsay slid closer to me across the leather seat. "She doesn't deserve you."

Now I really wanted to know what Luis told her about me.

Envy had just opened on Hollywood Boulevard. It was supposed to be the new VIP nightspot where only the *crème de la crème* constituted the guest list. Luis assured me our lack of invitation wouldn't be a problem. Tanya was impressed with him, and in turn, Lindsay was impressed with me. He pulled up to the curb and handed the valet a bill from his pocket without glancing at the denomination. He played the part of a socialite well.

On the sidewalk, a velvet rope partitioned a line of chicly dressed patrons spanning the block. Bass reverberated through the walls like soldiers marching with anvils for feet. The word "Envy," in rough scripted letters, had been cut from the hunk of steel mounted over the door. Green light permeated the missing metal and cast a menacing glow on the terrazzo and bronze Walk of Fame. The girls tried to suppress their excitement, to pretend as though this privileged access was routine. Meanwhile, I tried not to let on that this kind of place hadn't been my scene for years.

The bouncer's muscles indented folds in his black dress shirt. He firmly told the people in line they weren't getting in. Luis called out, "Charlie," and the bouncer's intimidating demeanor evaporated.

"Hey, Mr. Sanders. Good to see you again."

"Good to see you, Charlie. How's the scene look tonight?"

"It's a class act. How many?"

"Four." Luis handed him a couple fifties.

"Come on in." The metal clasp chimed as Charlie unhooked the rope. "Have you had a chance to listen to my band's demo?"

"It's at the top of my list. Don't worry. We'll talk soon."

"Thanks a lot, Mr. Sanders. Enjoy your evening."

The four of us walked under the sign and across the padded carpet. Groans filtered from the people in line much to the girls' delight.

Inside, white lamps sat on booth tabletops that stretched along the walls of the circular club. I recognized several people sitting or walking by from music or television or movies. Some I knew by name, others by sight. A golden rail separated the main level from the sunken dance floor where multitudes of indistinguishable people moved to the anvil beats. The VIP mezzanine skirted the upper walls above the DJ's loft. A red hourglass silhouette removed her top as she danced for someone sitting against the window.

"We'll be right back," Tanya said. "Why don't you

get us some drinks?"

Luis and I made our way to the bar and ordered champagne.

"Who'd you tell these girls we were?" I asked.

He laughed. "Record execs."

"Don't you think we're a little young to be executives?"

"They see the flash surrounding us and believe whatever they choose. Your dad works at Capitol, right? You know the lingo." He smacked my arm to punctuate his argument.

The female bartender lined up four flutes and poured the drinks. She gave Luis a flirtatious wink, her way of asking for a generous tip. He handed me a glass and raised another.

"Cheers," he said.

Once the girls returned, we finished a couple more drinks. Tanya danced in her seat until she couldn't take it anymore and pulled Luis toward the dance floor. Lindsay looked over to me, waiting to be invited next. I knew what she wanted but pretended I didn't. I already regretted having come. Soon enough, she grew tired of waiting and grabbed my hand.

She slithered a path through the crowd until she found an open pocket. She wrapped her arms around my neck, moved close against me. She swayed to the bassline as I slipped my hand over the small of her back. She lifted her half-drunken eyes from her cleavage to my face.

"How long have you been in the music business?"

It didn't matter what I said. I could afford being someone else tonight.

"Oh, several years. I discovered a lot of new talent

in business school at USC."

"Sounds exciting."

She ground her hips against mine. I was beginning to feel the champagne, so I responded in kind. She moved her face closer until we were almost nose-to-nose. Her eyes flirted even more than the rest of her body. The false intimacy made me feel desirable. Calm. For a moment I became preoccupied with the sensation.

I peeked over her shoulder to see Tanya frantically kissing Luis. She'd probably asked him similar, if not identical, questions. He definitely enjoyed himself. Lindsay's finger moved my chin to face her again. I felt her skirt stretch taut against my thigh.

"What happened with your girlfriend?"

I thought of the multitude of stories I could tell her, but I didn't want to talk about it. I told her so.

"She's got to be crazy if she doesn't want you. I could treat you better."

My eyes wandered over her shoulder to find something else to focus on. Before I knew what had happened, Lindsay's tongue searched my mouth for diamonds and hundred dollar bills. She looked in vain because there was no treasure. I didn't have the checkbook to sponsor my embellished claims. I'd been carried away by this personality I created, however briefly he existed, attaching myself to his coattails for the ride. Of course, he welcomed me along. He even insisted. But I didn't anticipate the awkward fit of a borrowed tuxedo. And Lindsay didn't understand the difference.

I grabbed her shoulders and moved her back. I didn't have anything to say to her. I simply walked out of the club.

CHAPTER THIRTY-THREE

A cab took me home. I couldn't even remember the last time I sat in one of these things with their competing odors of cigarette smoke and Armor All. Not having an accessible car in LA was a form of emasculation. I writhed with this thought the entire ride home, the cherry on top of today's shit sundae.

In my apartment's garage, the Mustang was a comforting sight for about two seconds. Then I remembered the car would be the only familiarity welcoming me home tonight.

I popped the trunk since I hadn't brought my suitcase upstairs earlier. Unpacking would at least give me a task to complete. I struggled to free the luggage, but something held the baggage down. I pulled with enough force to bring it a foot closer. I tried again. Nothing. Frustrated, I dropped the case. I reached in to find the rope Alex had bought at David's hardware store was tangled around my suitcase wheels.

That's when I stopped.

Alex.

What the hell have I done?

I pulled, pulled until the wheels spun free. I ripped the chord from the trunk, raveled it into a ball, and threw it across the parking garage. The end tangled around my finger, stopping the rope's flight. I flung the rest on the ground and kicked and yelled at the knotted mass.

I hated driving. I didn't want to do it anymore. I'd done enough of it today. This week.

I hated driving. But I had to start the engine.

I repeated these words like a mantra over and over as I threw the shifter into gear.

I'm never driving again.

SATURDAY

CHAPTER THIRTY-FOUR

I drove back to Lone Pine like a maniac. I didn't know what time it was. I didn't care. My only objective was to race as quickly as possible without hitting anything on the darkened road. When I felt my attention wane, my teeth ripped the plastic seal from another Frappuccino bottle, and I downed the boost of caffeine. If these vanilla coffees had powered me through countless all-nighters in college, they could get me back to Lone Pine.

I tried to shake off thinking as well, which proved difficult. The cuts remained on Alex's wrist, and the apple slice of a scar still burned on his hip. None of them would even be there if it weren't for me.

Misgivings ground against my conscience like rusted gears. The friction hurt my teeth. I was probably too late. I'd committed the worst error possible by leaving. I was certain all I had to drive back to was my friend's corpse floating in bloody bathwater.

I couldn't allow it. I wouldn't. I wouldn't make the same mistake again.

I pressed harder against the pedal.

*　*　*

The familiar arrow of yellow lights directed me to the Trails Motel. It felt like forever since I'd been here when I'd only left this morning. The night air was cold after a week of heat. I ran to room seven and pounded on the door. No answer. I tried peering through the drapes, but they were drawn and the lights were off. My fist hammered again on the door. I quickly patted my jacket pockets, found the motel key, and stabbed the metal into the lock.

The room was empty; yet his clothes were still here. I flicked on the bathroom light. The mirror was broken. Reflective shards littered the countertop. Blood clotted on the corner of a glass triangle the size of a tortilla chip. I found no crimson puddles anywhere. I looked to the bathtub, flung open the shower curtain.

No Alex. Only spotless porcelain.

I called his cell for the eighty-seventh time. Nothing was more frustrating than knowing I couldn't get a hold of him when the phone lived in his pocket.

I ran to the front desk to find the old man with Coke-bottle glasses. I tapped on the bell in rapid fire to wake him from his nap. He jolted upward. The copy of *Time* magazine fell from his stomach to the floor.

"Excuse me. I'm staying in room seven. Have you seen the guy I came here with?"

The old man searched his memory.

"You recommended the ghost town to him," I added.

"Oh, him. He came in, um, about an hour ago."

Thank God he was still alive—at least he was an hour ago.

"He asked for me to call him a cab. I told him it'd take a while to get one here, so he started walking."

"Did he say where he was going?"

"Nope. You should probably try his cell phone."

I searched the night sky for where he could have possibly gone in a town with a single traffic light. I pulled my car back onto Main Street, hoping I'd run into him. Then again, if he'd left an hour ago, he could be anywhere and possibly not even on a road. I searched for a bar or anything that might still be open at this hour.

Nothing.

My only chance was a small light on the hill.

CHAPTER THIRTY-FIVE

Gravel crunched beneath my tires as the Frankenstein House appeared atop the steep driveway. All the lights were ablaze. Heavy shadows stretched from under the eves and crawled over the ground. David's car rested in its usual spot, but a maroon Explorer I hadn't seen before was parked directly behind at a crooked angle. He was going to be thrilled to see me. "Yes, hi, sorry to bother you. I've lost your son. You know, the one you never want to see again? Any chance he's lying around here?"

This should be great.

I looked in the windows. Someone was definitely home. Raised voices mumbled from inside. I saw a man's back that had to be David's. His body covered the other person, who's verbal bashing he tried to avoid. David yelled, "No, no," and he and the visitor moved toward the kitchen. The shift in bodies revealed Alex sitting behind them on the edge of the couch. His leather wristband had been re-strapped. I had to credit his stubbornness for not going down without a fight.

I leapt onto the front porch and tried the door

handle. The latch clicked under my finger. Compared to the cold night, the living room was almost unbearably hot. The sauna atmosphere knocked me back like a pungent odor. Flames crackled in the brick fireplace. That's when I recognized the second, belligerent voice. Matt Morgan swayed in and out of the kitchen doorway.

"You stole her from me," Matt said. "You stole her and you never apologized."

"I'm sorry," David replied. "Does that make you happy? I'm sorry."

Alex, with great interest, watched the brothers battle. Kiana spied on them from her favorite couch, where she'd curled up to escape the argument. She didn't even raise her head when I walked in.

"Alex," I whispered. "Alex."

He turned. Unexpected relief swept over me when I saw him move. He was real. His eyes widened for a second. He raised a finger to his mouth, then turned back to David and Matt. I scowled at his demand for my silence. I crossed the hardwood floor to reach him.

"He just wants to talk," Matt said. "You owe him that. If Annie were here, she'd help him out. He's not just her kid. I don't want to ever hear you say that again."

I was drawn into what sounded like parents fighting over their child. I asked Alex, "What did I miss?"

"I came here to talk to David. Matt showed up right after."

"Has he been drinking?"

"Yuuup."

David seemed even more shaken by his brother's attacks when he noticed that I had joined the party. Matt followed his frown to me.

"Look," Matt said. "We need to figure this out. We need to find common ground here."

"Common ground?" David said.

"Yes."

"Level the playing field?"

"Exactly."

"Best idea you had all night." David opened an upper cabinet and pulled out a half-empty bottle of Jack Daniel's. He tilted it in our direction. "Whiskey?"

Alex and I shook our heads.

He poured three fingers into a lowball glass and downed the liquor as if it were water. He poured himself a refill.

Alex stood up. "I don't think that's going to help anything."

David brought the bottle out of the kitchen. He pointed the glass at Alex when he passed him, spilling some of the alcohol as he said, "Don't presume to know what happened."

He continued into the living room. He looked as though he might head upstairs. Instead, he stopped in the center of the house where the country living room, Spanish family room, and lumber storage space all met.

Alex squared off to his back. "We can argue forever over who's to blame. Get over it." He directed his comment at both brothers. "Let's figure this out."

"Enough," David yelled, spinning around, throwing the whiskey bottle. The jug missed the brick of the hearth and landed in the fire, breaking a log and igniting the alcohol. Kiana bolted from the couch to safety. The flare puffed outward rather harmlessly, but the falling log set fire to the rug.

The quarrel stopped immediately. The four of

us jumped to alerted stations, and we scrambled in different directions with a new purpose. David stomped on the fire with his boot. Alex batted the flames with throw pillows. I ran to fill a pitcher with water, but dousing the blaze had little effect.

Matt came in next with a small fire extinguisher from under the kitchen sink. The safety pin was stuck. The flames crept to the couch by the time Matt pulled the pin free. He pushed down the trigger, and white foam sputtered from the nozzle. He checked the pressure gauge.

"This doesn't work," he said.

David looked around. "I have a full size extinguisher around here somewhere."

David and Alex ran to the storage room while I called 911. The fire spread to the front curtains. Matt leapt onto the couch, the flames licking his feet. He ripped the curtains from their rods. He bundled the unburned fabric as much as possible and tossed it into the fireplace. He'd halted the vertical spread, but the couch continued to be eaten. His feet danced around the cushions to avoid the heat.

David and Alex climbed over ladders and around tool chests. They looked under painting tarps and behind stacks of wood

Matt jumped back on the floor. "Forget the extinguisher. Let's go."

Then David shouted, "Found it."

A crash shortened the celebration.

I turned around to see a mountain of lumber falling from the corner. The wood pummeled father and son, causing the red extinguisher to hit the floor.

Matt and I raced to the back room. Alex and David

lay motionless under the pile. We pulled the boards off. A splinter jammed between my thumb and forefinger. My teeth clenched at the pain, but I continued to work. They groaned as we relieved the pressure on top of them. They were battered but semi-conscious.

The flames rose behind us, up toward the TV secured above the mantel. I'd begun to sweat from the heat.

Matt kicked the fire extinguisher aside; then he locked his hands under his brother's arms and pulled him up. I did the same with Alex. He was able to walk if he leaned against me.

"This way," Matt said.

He slung David's arm over his shoulder. I followed him toward the back door, away from the smoke. We lurched across the floor of the outside sunroom. Our feet shuffled over patches of sawdust. I heard Kiana barking somewhere nearby. She was already safe outside and waiting for us. Matt and David made their way down the back steps as Alex tripped over a circular saw. He fell forward, taking me with him. I hit my eye on the concrete porch. We scrambled to our feet only to tumble down the remaining steps.

The buckle of Alex's wristband broke against the ground. He grabbed his hand in pain while I tried to dig out the tearing sensation from my shoulder. We both lay on the cold dirt—unglamorously incapacitated— behind the house consumed from within.

CHAPTER THIRTY-SIX

Matt and I sat in the lobby of Southern Inyo Hospital. My arm hung in a sling while my face felt contorted by painkillers and a back porch.

Matt had escaped unharmed, except his clothes gave off a slightly charred smell. Or that might have been me. He crossed his arms one chair over. Frustration had made him quite sober.

David finally emerged from the patients' area. He averted his eyes on his way to the front door. Matt jumped up and grabbed his arm.

"Where are you going?"

He didn't want to answer, almost as if the words pained him.

"I have to go," he said.

He continued forward. Matt went after him. They stopped just outside, trying to speak in hushed tones that only clarified every syllable.

"You're just leaving?" Matt said. "What about Alex?"

"I already told him. There's nothing left for me here now. I'm selling my half of the store to Tom."

"How can we help you out? Tell me what I can do."

David shook his head. "I can't." He looked up at Matt, fully earnest. "I'm sorry." He glanced at me one last time, then disappeared around the corner.

Matt called after him. He ran his fingers through his hair, watching David walk away. No one knew where he was going. David probably didn't even know. He just had to move. I pictured he and his dog heading down a lonely, desert highway in search of a new home, a place to start over even farther away from his family. I guess that was his choice.

Matt returned to the chair beside me, churning over what might be the last time he'll see David in who knows how long.

"You okay?" I asked.

Matt exhaled. "He's not a bad guy. He just has a lot to figure out."

I shifted to relieve my shoulder's discomfort.

"Is it true that you were going to marry Annie?"

A thought carried him away from the hospital. Still staring into other times he said, "I was ready. She wasn't. Annie was a very confused person. Didn't really know herself then. She thought committing to David after her slip up was best for Alex.

"Still," he mused, "after all that, as much as he and I don't get along, he is my brother."

"You don't have to tell me everything," I said.

"Alex should know. I also want him to know he can call me if he needs anything."

"He'll appreciate that."

Matt patted my healthy shoulder the way a father would.

Just then, the doctor entered. I approached as soon

as I saw her, my anxiety contrasting the controlled demeanor that physicians must study to perfect.

"Alex has a sprained wrist," she said.

"That's it?" I said. "It's not broken?"

"He just needs to ice it and keep it wrapped." She directed her attention to the bruise on my face. "What about you? Any headaches? I really would like to get an X-ray."

I moved from under her scrutiny. "It's just a black eye. I've had them before. When can I see him?"

She accepted my refusal.

"He's asking for you."

The doctor directed me to room 102. I read the plate several times just to verify I had the correct door. I procrastinated some more by studying the Braille translation underneath.

Alex sat alone in the far corner bed. He looked out the windows where the first streaks of a cloudy sunrise stabbed over the mountains. My eyes shot to his wrist cradled over his lap, wrapped in an ACE bandage. I ventured two steps. He turned. The scratches on his face matched the ones on mine.

Embarrassment crossed his eyes, and he turned back to the window. I continued forward, measuring each pace with a jagged breath. I didn't dare get closer than the foot of his bed.

"David gone?" he asked.

I nodded. I rolled the folds of his bed sheets between my fingers. Alex seemed ambivalent, almost content with the outcome. He licked his lips.

"Ashley called to wish me a happy birthday."

"That's good."

"Brian and Meghan didn't." He shrugged off the thought. "They're preoccupied."

"They're not perfect." I waited to see if he'd respond. He didn't. "I have to admit... When Shannon and I split several years ago, I was really into Meghan. Which was crazy because she was never going to leave Brian. She'd always come by the apartment, you know? It's just, I've had this idea that you and I could date girls who were best friends. Maybe even marry them someday. That way we'd have this group for holidays, vacations, our kids playing together."

His apprehension turned to sympathy. He faced me with no resistance in his eyes.

"Now you know what I had in Seattle."

Something inside me clicked. For all the reasons I'd spewed at him to forget about those people, he knew exactly what he stood to lose. Or regain. I think I understood him for the first time. I felt centered— although a bit transparent. He seemed to know everything I thought, nodding at each bite-sized revelation that crossed my mind.

"So what now?" I asked.

"Now," he said, "I have to fix my marriage."

I breathed deeply. "I thought you needed time to figure stuff out on your own."

"I did. When you took off earlier, I spent hours sorting everything out." He smiled. "That was the best thing you could have done. Really. I needed a good kick in the ass."

I had a hard time wrapping my brain around what he was telling me.

"What changed?" I asked. "Why keep trying?"

He shrugged.

"I care about her. Isn't that enough?"

He bowed his head. The corner of his mouth began to turn up until he laughed to himself.

"What's so funny?" I asked.

He relished his thought a moment longer.

"Ashley does this thing when she sleeps, where her hand moves to scratch her nose. The first night we spent together, I woke up all of a sudden…dazed… because she'd socked me in the face."

I tried not to snicker. "Maybe you should have taken that as a sign."

"No, it was cute. One time I wasn't asleep when I saw her hand begin to move. I grabbed it so she couldn't reach her nose. She never woke up, but her hand kept struggling."

He never seemed happier than when he was with Ashley. The same pleasure even sparked when he spoke of her. He knew it, and now I knew it: Alex was his best self with her.

"So what are you going to do?" I asked.

"No idea."

"It's not going to be easy."

"I know."

I believed he understood the difficulty of his next task. His success depended on how Ashley worked with him. But again, he always was a stubborn guy.

"Thanks," he continued. "For tonight. The week. I had a good time."

I huffed.

"I've had better."

CHAPTER THIRTY-SEVEN

L one Pine to LA. LAX to Sea-Tac. Interstate 5 to Alex's house. I was a passenger the whole way. I'd kept true to my promise that I'd never drive again. I had tossed Alex my keys as soon as Matt drove us back to the car. We said our goodbyes. He gave Alex his info. Alex reimbursed the motel for the bathroom mirror. After boarding a plane that afternoon, we were back in Seattle by an overcast Saturday evening.

Ashley wasn't there. She and the bridesmaids had planned a whole event the night before the wedding. She was probably staying with Meghan anyway.

I tried my shoulder without the sling. The soreness was manageable as I placed two steaming cups of tea on the kitchen table. I sat down and tested the chamomile with my lips. Alex was busy creating a mosaic of colors on his ACE bandage. He was about to fill in the remaining space near his thumb when the marker ground to a halt. He stared at the wrapping for a moment as something flashed in his eyes. He dropped the pen and almost knocked over his chair as he stood.

He rounded the corner to open his art studio's

pocket doors. Inside, I found him facing the canvas on the easel.

The portrait of Ashley.

He seized his paints and brushes and cleared some room to work, which was when I knew he no longer saw me. He began with the red streak across her face that was once an accident, now an incorporation. Instead of masking the hole punched through the back, he accentuated the void as if chaos erupted from the breach. He organized the bedlam, allowing each focal point to transition to the next. A pattern resembling waves crashed in the bottom left corner. He exaggerated the scar on her cheek and her extra smile line on the other side. Fire erupted over her head. Music notes danced across her chest. Apples grew on a tree behind her shoulder. Next to the tear rose two monoliths in the Eastern sky where, at their base, lay a broken ring fused together. The emotions of the entire week exploded onto the canvas in a flurry of reds and shadows.

When evening eventually succumbed to night, I turned on the house lamps. He looked around at the sudden change in atmosphere but dismissed the observation. He didn't stop painting once. From what began as a portrait gentle enough for an aristocrat's parlor emerged a furious return of Alex's inherent style.

Midnight chimed. He carefully set down his brush and palette, then staggered backward from the canvas. He'd tied the various elements into what came to be a solid image. He admired the brush strokes. Her textured skin. The exploding stars. He stepped back once more and fell next to me on the velvet chaise beneath the window. He exhaled as if it were his first breath in hours.

"I'm hungry," he said.

"I'll bet."

I closed the copy of *Smithsonian* I'd found in the stack of mail by the front door. Alex looked at me for the first time since daylight.

"I think I have some pasta in the fridge," he said.

"I ate that hours ago while watching reruns of *Colbert* and *The Daily Show*."

"Oh." He looked surprised that the TV was once on. "Well then...let's go out."

As we stood up, something fell out the magazine in my hand. It was a letter. I picked up the envelope and stopped when I read the address.

"Alex?"

He, too, looked shocked when he saw the name John Kemp of Levant Street, San Francisco. Alex ripped open the seal. Inside was a note that reported how John had sifted through some storage items and found a picture of Annie that Alex might like to have. Paper-clipped to the back was a photo of his mother, the first real image he had ever seen of her.

The picture was a close-up, taken from an intimate distance. She stared straight into the camera, her dark hair framing her pale skin, freckled nose, and murky blue eyes. Alex examined the image in silence. Then his mouth formed the sad grin I've seen a thousand times before, the same smile Annie had in the photo.

But that wasn't the final surprise of the evening.

Upstairs, Alex headed to his bedroom for a change of clothes. From the closet door hung a black garment bag with a pink Post-it note stuck to the outside. The markered cursive read, "Miss you."

Inside rested the best man tuxedo.

A NEW WEEK

CHAPTER THIRTY-EIGHT

Alex and I approached the church in Edmonds—me in my pinstripe suit, he in his classic black tuxedo, bow tie, and vest. The ceremony was about to start any minute. We crossed the first set of double doors into a carpeted foyer, where the groomsmen escorted guests to their seats. Brian, dressed in the same tux with a white vest and bow tie, happily greeted one person after another before the doors to the main hall. He stood tall among his family and friends. His broad shoulders were thrown back so that his posture matched his rented elegance. Even after all these years, I still didn't know how his hair remained perfectly gelled all the time.

He did a double take when he saw Alex and me. He left his post and crossed straight to us, his pleasure overwhelming his shock. "You made it." He hugged us both. I congratulated him on his wedding day, which he acknowledged only with a quick thank you. Something more important preoccupied his thoughts.

"I've been a shitty friend," he said to Alex. "Goodness, what happened to your face?"

Alex waved his hand to say forget about it. "Where's Eric?"

Brian frowned more as a formality since he'd already accepted the result. "A job opportunity came up and he took it. He's gone again. But that doesn't matter. I shouldn't have done what I did. I should have—"

Alex cut him off. "We'll have plenty of time to talk about that later. Right now, let's just get you married."

Brian's eyes convinced me of his sincerity. Even his slick-talking charisma couldn't lie that well. Like Alex had said, Brian's earlier behavior must have stemmed from a weakness of character—perhaps a serious lapse in judgment—but not from malice. I chose to believe that.

A commotion rattled behind us, and Brian lost his status as the main attraction. The bridal party entered from a side door. She stepped into the lobby just then: the maid of honor. Alex's composure broke when he noticed Ashley in her black satin dress and white sash hugging her waist.

She stopped when she saw her husband for the first time in a week. A gentle smile found its way to the corners of her mouth, which turned to concern as she stepped closer. She touched the scrapes around his eye. Her chin shook, which accentuated her uneven smile lines. Her fingers hovered above his bandaged wrist before she drew back and dipped them into his healthy hand. He rotated her wedding ring in a full circle. She wanted to speak but couldn't find the words.

Jacqueline, in her matching bridesmaid dress, watched from behind. Her lips assumed their trademark smirk. She stepped forward. Going shoulder to shoulder, I grabbed her arm.

"Leave it alone," I said. "It won't work out the way you want."

While unhappy with my interruption, her grin remained. I couldn't help but feel she was impressed with my play, but just the same, she could have been telling me I only changed her plans today. I hoped my first thought was correct.

The organ began. The wedding party lined up. I was about to head inside when Ashley, still unable to speak, came over and gave me a hug. Her glassy eyes thanked me enough.

Brian headed down the aisle, cuing Meghan to join the end of the procession. White flowers dotted her long hair. Her clean-lined dress with beaded detail resembled Ashley's wedding gown. Leave it to best friends to share similar tastes. Her excitement was only heightened when Ashley presented Alex. He and the bride shared a firm embrace.

I used the opportunity to carve out space in an off-center pew. A few people stared at my bruised eye. For a moment I considered telling them how I got it. Instead, I stood with my shoulders straight and one hand holding the other in front.

The wedding party began down the aisle. Right together, left together. I recognized the bride and groom's various friends from high school and college. Meghan's younger brother, a short but built Italian, walked with Jacqueline. Her gaze knew exactly where to find me. She held my eyes until she could no longer see me without straining her neck.

Not far behind, Alex and Ashley returned to the site of their own ceremony. Her blond curls, despite being pinned up, bounced ever so slightly as she walked left together, right together toward the altar, her arm wrapped around the elbow of the reinstated best man. They both grinned. Right together, left together. She lost her rhythm for just a second when their eyes met. I doubt anyone else in the church caught the moment. I did. I also was the only one among them who understood the full significance of her smile.

CHAPTER THIRTY-NINE

The Fairmont Olympic Hotel was a downtown Seattle landmark. A gold-banistered staircase and plush red carpeting led the way through the enormous double doors of the Spanish Ballroom, flourished with ornate details and luxurious curtains draping the two-story windows. Brian always surrounded himself with the finer things, especially when it came to his wife. He raised a champagne flute to the applause of two hundred guests.

I'd been squeezed into Brian's family table next to the dance floor, which happened to be the closest seats to Ashley and Alex on their elevated wedding party station. He snuck glances at her during the groom's toast.

Meghan accepted the microphone next.

"I just wanted to thank all our friends who flew up here to be with us. Laura and Jennifer, Graham and Ed..." She looked around the room at each one until her smile focused on the person to her left. "And Alex, and Alex, and Alex," she repeated, patting his shoulder each time she said his name.

* * *

After the reception, the Seattle crew climbed into Ashley's beat-up, white station wagon at the hotel valet station. The girls had changed out of their dresses. Whatever their destination, I felt vindicated that the bride and groom took time out of their wedding night to welcome Alex back into the fold.

Meghan's brother handed Brian a duffle bag, which he snuck into the car's trunk. The design looked familiar, but his effort to conceal it didn't give me the proper chance to see. They were ready to take off. I saluted Alex in the passenger seat.

He told Ashley to wait. Everyone in the car exchanged a few words before Alex opened his door and said, "Come on, boy. Jump in."

I frowned but joined them anyway. "What am I? The family dog?"

Instead of squeezing in the front, I scooted into the backseat with Brian and Meghan. We were on our way out of downtown.

"Where are we going?" Alex asked.

"You'll see." Ashley exchanged conspiratorial nods with the newly weds. Everyone was in on the secret except Alex and me.

Brian tried to navigate. "Turn right. No, left. Maybe it's the next street. Okay, this looks familiar. Wait. Maybe not." We drove in circles through a residential neighborhood backed by evergreens. Ashley slammed on the breaks in the middle of the intersection and demanded, "Make up your mind."

After a few moments, he regained his bearings. "It's this way."

The houses slowly disappeared. More trees filled the landscape until we were driving through a wooded glen. Sunlight filtered through the treetops and freckled the car windshield. I still hadn't gotten used to how late the sun lingered this time of year.

She pulled off on a secluded dirt road. The car bobbed along the uneven path, pebbles popping under the tires. A chain-link fence materialized between the trees. Then, blue bleachers, a red backstop, and a diamond—the traditional sort with infield grass and sunken dugouts.

"What's summer without a little baseball?" Brian said. He stepped out of the car and pulled the bag Meghan's brother had handed him before we left. As it turned out, he'd been sent on an errand to fetch his coaching bag from the car. Gloves, bats, and balls filled the duffle. Brian tossed me a weathered mitt. "What do you say, Ed?"

Ashley bounced back and forth like a boxer, attempting to intimidate Alex.

"We're not dressed for a game," I said.

Meghan shrugged. "So?"

"Well, you are. You're not wearing your dress anymore."

"I would have. It's not like I'm ever going to wear it again. *She* made me change."

"You just can't do that to a dress," Ashley said.

Brian and Alex took off their jackets and bow ties. I followed suit. I hadn't played in a couple years. The feel of the leather in my hand was comforting. I said to Brian, "I hope you can play ball better than you give directions."

Meghan laughed, and Brian joked, "You better

watch it, Cohen."

Alex and Ashley played against each other but soon ended up on the same team. He and I had a stint together, too—that was until he relieved Brian to pitch to me the way he used to after games and practices back when we first met. He wasn't a pitcher by any means. He invented overdramatic strides that made me laugh so hard I missed the pitch altogether. I threw the ball back saying, "Pitch it the right way," only to have him do something even more absurd.

Then it began to rain. I ran into the dugout for cover from the sudden showers.

"Where you going?" he asked.

"Angelenos don't like rain."

"You're not the family dog. You're a cat."

The four of them continued playing even harder as though the water had revitalized them. Ashley cracked a ball into right field and ran with gusto around the bases. Alex didn't even bother fielding the hit. He charged after her, and she squealed with delight. He picked her up. Her legs kicked as she spun. She kept saying she had to make it to the next base, reaching out with her fingers to get there faster. Meghan snuck up, tickled him until Ashley was free. Alex let his wife relish her trip around the field, and he smiled proudly as Brian put his arm around him. That's when it hit me.

He was home.

CHAPTER FORTY

Ashley dropped me off at the hotel so she and Alex could be alone tonight. I plodded across the lobby in my drenched suit. The desk clerk looked at me strangely when I asked him to direct me someplace warm, preferably with music and a bar.

Jazz Alley was a couple blocks away. The entrance was literally in the alley between 5th and 6th Avenues. I must have been a sight: a well-dressed stranger soaked from head to toe. My tie hung loosely around my neck and my shoes left a trail of size ten puddles.

A soulful trio performed their rendition of "Route 66." One feature I liked most about jazz were the standards. Fifty different artists could play the same song fifty different ways and each version was like hearing the tune for the first time.

I sat in the back corner the darkened club, sipping a whiskey sour. My thumbs tapped my thighs along to the drummer brushing the cymbals. Each tap cleared my head a little more. I didn't mind sitting alone, but I thought of someone who would enjoy being here, too. I dialed.

"Hey, dad. Guess where I am."

"Where?"

"Jazz Alley."

"Wow. I haven't been there in, probably, twenty years."

"It's my first time. It's great."

I left the club and the rain began again. I was already dirty. I expected some hard-nosed questions from the dry cleaner later. This time, though, I didn't mind the shower.

I wondered what Alex was up to, whether he and Ashley were talking or simply falling asleep together, listening to each other breathe. At first I didn't understand why he'd been so loyal to the Seattleites, but once they were there for him when he needed people most. That counted for something. I thought of his face in the rain while I watched from tonight's dugout—the same smile from when we rode on Brian's fishing boat all those years ago.

"Don't worry, Ed," Brian's dad had called from the helm. "I've seen weather much worse than this."

I tried to steady myself in the dining nook as the Tollycraft sloshed through the waters of Puget Sound. Alex and Brian stood beyond the cabin door, using their distributed body weight to balance the boat, cheering and laughing after each swell they overcame.

"How much farther?" I asked.

"What?" they answered in unison.

"Land. When is land?"

But Alex kept on smiling.

Yes.

And back at the dock, Ashley hurried down the ramp and leapt into his arms. She kissed him all over his face before locking his bottom lip between hers. She missed him, hated being away from him if only for a day. She could never be just a girl—the same way that afternoon would never be just a day.

He smiled the night he met Ashley, when we returned to campus and she kicked off her shoes and rolled up her jeans before jumping in the shallow fountain outside the engineering school. Meghan laughed and said, "Will someone get her?" Alex hopped toward the water, peeling off his last sock and carefully stepping to avoid slipping. He fell anyway and submerged in the foot-deep pool.

We all erupted with laughter when he surfaced, his mouth dropped in astonishment. Yes. And I'm certain he smiled when he and Ashley stole away to her backseat when she first said, "I'm going to marry you someday," and the rain fell harder.

Seattle rain wasn't like those random LA drops, the midnight ones outside our college apartment when Alex and I shared Chicago-style crust with our girls. All the while, the rain pattered against the window like the sound of Shannon running around the dirt track the day we met through a chain-link fence.

But the track. Yeah. The track is what I'll always remember. If I could paint like Alex, that would be my portrait: Shannon running alongside me the day we met, when her hazel eyes filled with the hope of a relationship not yet tested by time and discord. Still, while that purity was worth defending, her expression that day didn't convey the strength gained from both the dark times as well as the light—the look she had as we drank wine on the kitchen floor and talked till dawn, or when we hugged for the first time after a fight.

I'd say that look in her eyes was worth even more. I owed it to her to keep the fire alive. What's more, I owed it to myself.

"What are you doing in Seattle?" my dad asked on the phone. "You there much longer?"

I wasn't. The next morning I was on a flight back to LA. As for my first order of business, I gave my boss my resignation.

"What'll you do?" he asked.

"I'll figure out something."

Next I gave my landlord notice, and days later I watched the moving men park my car inside the Mayflower truck. They filled the rest of the cargo bed with my clothes, furniture, and the remainder of Shannon's belongings until the apartment was empty.

I hadn't called her yet. She didn't know I was coming. I wanted to surprise her by finally answering her question in person.

Back at LAX for a record sixth time in two weeks, while looking for my printed confirmation in my computer bag, I found the caricature Alex had drawn in the motel room. My cartoon self juggled my laptop, telephone, him, and Shannon. As if Alex knew I was thinking of him at that moment, he texted me.

"Good luck," the message read. "Don't be a stranger."

"Sir, can I help you?"

The airline attendant waited behind the counter. I slid my luggage forward and handed her the flight confirmation.

"To Baltimore," I said. "One way."

ACKNOWLEDGEMENTS

This book has taken on more than a dozen shapes through the years, and the final result has been improved, in large part, by several wonderful people. First, I would like to thank my fiction professors who helped turn night into day on more than one occasion: Patty Seyburn, TC Boyle, SL Stebel, Aram Saroyan, Rachel Resnick, John Rechy, and Shelly Lowenkopf. Second, I am indebted to my trusted friends and family who have offered their time and valuable feedback: Kim, Robin, and Mike Gardina, Don and Joyce Marie Brusasco, Eduardo Mendoza, Alex Macias, Meghan Zuck, Mat Morgan, Kelly McDonald, and my peers in both the USC Professional Writing Program and the USC English department. Third, and certainly not least, I'd like to thank you, reader, for picking up a copy of my first novel. You are the reason I wrote this book in the first place.

ABOUT THE AUTHOR

Daniel Gardina is a Los Angeles-based writer who earned his BA and MFA from the University of Southern California. He is the author of *The Lookout and Other Stories* as well as the *Hollywood Novelist* blog. This is his first novel.

Learn more at danielgardina.com.

www.ingramcontent.com/pod-product-compliance
Lightning Source LLC
Chambersburg PA
CBHW070814180626
46818CB00001B/266